Authority Issues

PHOEBE ALEXANDER

MOUNTAINS WANTED
PUBLISHING & INDIE AUTHOR SERVICES

 Created with Vellum

Authority Issues

Shea Hunt has an attitude problem that started when he was a kid. When he's fired for insubordination and returns to college to pursue his dream career, there is one class standing in the way of him getting into business school: an intensive writing course. And the professor teaching it just happens to be a girl he teased mercilessly in high school.

Dr. Zara Ames can hardly believe her eyes when one of the students in her intensive writing class is none other than her high school bully. It's hard to put those painful memories behind her and offer him the extra help he needs to pass the course.

When the two grow closer than either anticipated, will Zara's bid for tenure be thwarted by her lecherous department chair? And will Shea prove he's never quite gotten past his authority issues?

Prologue

THEIR LAUGHTER ECHOED in my head long after I walked away from the scene in the cafeteria. My tray of food lay spilled across the dingy tiled floor. Mashed potatoes in a smushy lump with peas scattered for yards. A stiff piece of breaded chicken—or it was *supposed* to be chicken, anyway—lay askew next to a puddle of syrupy peaches.

"What's wrong, Zara? Not hungry anymore?" his voice taunted as I kept walking, my face red with rage and tears brimming in my eyes. I could walk all the way to Canada, and no one would care.

A janitor appeared out of nowhere, armed with a long broom, and brushed past me, his eyes trained on the mess I'd left in the middle of the cafeteria floor. A momentary flash of guilt rifled through me, knowing I was leaving that mess for him to clean up, but it wasn't my fault Shea Hunt knocked my tray out of my hands when he told me fat cows shouldn't be eating so much.

Next thing I knew, I was locking myself in the last stall in the bathroom, the dusky pink metal door scratched with graffiti blurring as the tears finally overwhelmed me and began to spill down my face. I couldn't go to class like this. I would have to go to the school nurse and feign a headache or cramps or something. They'd never question cramps, if I was brave enough to claim that was what ailed me.

It meant asking my father to come pick me up, though. My mother was a teacher at the nearby elementary school, and she couldn't just leave in the middle of the day.

When you choose lying to your father and telling him you have cramps rather than going back to class...

Things had gone from bad to worse. And if I told my parents I was being bullied about my weight, they'd probably tell me I deserved it. That no one would ever love me the way I was.

I had already begun to believe it.

One

Zara

"READY FOR THIS?" came a nasal-sounding man's voice, irritating my ears.

I glanced up to find the chair of my department, Alan Palmer, staring at me with a smug smirk on his face. His shaved head gleamed under the lights as he stroked his long, narrow fingers down his gray goatee.

"Always," I answered, matching his smirk with one of my own.

He was the type of creature you couldn't show any weakness to, the type, who, if you gave an inch, he took a mile. I had learned the hard way not to give him a millimeter, let alone an inch. He'd been the chair of the English department for the last three years, and from what I understood, he had our dean, Cheryl Silva, wrapped around his finger.

"Full load this semester?" He continued leering at me,

his icy gray eyes traveling down my face toward my breasts. A creepy tingle danced up my spine as I crossed my arms over my chest to cover up.

"Yes." I grabbed a stack of files off my desk and rolled back in my chair. Rising to my sensible kitten heels, my nostrils flared as I tried to maintain a pleasant demeanor. "I need to get going. Don't want to be late on the first day."

"Good plan, Zara," he agreed, watching me hook my purse strap over my shoulder and grab my sweater from the back of the chair. My first class was in a drafty room in the basement of the humanities building.

"Have a good day, Alan." I brushed past him, but I could feel his hot stare burning into my ass as I walked away.

Everyone jokingly called the top floor of our building The Ivory Tower. As I approached the elevator, I stopped in front of the massive window at the top of the stairs. My gaze swept across campus. The view was thrilling from the fifth floor.

After a long hot summer, students were starting to trickle into campus for the start of the fall semester. It was going to be a good year; I could feel it. I was up for my tenure promotion, and I was confident after publishing my first book last spring I had a good shot at it. It was a book of poetry—not rigorous academic research like some of my colleagues had done, but it still counted toward my tenure activities.

The students were tiny from this vantage. Jeans, t-shirts, backpacks, fresh faces. They looked like harmless little ants scurrying around to get to their first classes of the day. When I began teaching, I was a little intimidated by the scowling faces of college students who didn't want to take a writing class, but after six years in this position, I'd found my stride. I loved instilling a bit of terror in my students on the first day.

I pressed the down elevator button and tapped my toe on the tile as I waited for the door to slide open. It was time to sharpen my claws and make a good—and by that I meant *scary*—first impression.

* * *

The students filtered in as I scanned the network drive for my PowerPoint with my lecture notes. They hated it when professors kept them the full class period on Day One, but I just loved the looks on their faces when they realized I was actually planning to teach them something from the get-go. I supposed that made me just a tiny bit sadistic, but I had so few pleasures in life. *Why shouldn't torturing my students— even just a little bit—be one of them?*

I was expecting thirty, which was bigger than I liked for a composition class, but I would make do. Likely a few would drop after this first day anyway, when they realized they would need to work their asses off to pass. Getting an A would require a shit ton of work. They didn't call it *intensive* writing for nothing.

The best part of this class? Business majors needed a passing grade to gain acceptance into business school. I always had a contingent of cocky business students who thought they could just waltz in here, jot down some steaming pile of shit, turn it in and pass. Um, no. It didn't work like that.

"Dr. Ames?" a tiny voice trembled from behind me.

I whipped around, eyes narrowed. "Yes?"

A petite blonde stood in front of me, nervously clutching a notebook to her chest. "Hi, I'm Becca Stanley. I was wondering if you could sign this add form from my advisor? I'm trying to add the class."

"The class is full; I'm sorry." My eyes traveled back down to my notebook where I had my lesson plan mapped out.

"Please?" She gave me puppy dog eyes. "I really need this class so I can get into the business school in the spring. I couldn't take it last spring because I did a semester abroad in Italy, and now I'm a junior, and I—"

See what I mean? A bunch of entitled pains in the asses, these students. Apparently I was supposed to open up a new seat in my class because she went to Italy last semester. For fuck's sake.

"Someone will probably drop after this session," I explained, "so you can add it then. But I cannot create an extra space for you."

I swear she stamped her little gladiator-sandaled foot, outraged I wouldn't bend the rules for her. "But my advisor said you could!"

I bit my bottom lip, stopping myself before I advised her to shut her mouth and go sit her little entitled ass down before it became acquainted with my foot. "Sorry, I don't make the rules." I managed to subdue my annoyance at her whiny little pathetic face staring up at me.

"I'll just have to get my parents to call," she huffed as she flounced out of the room.

I ignored her, not really giving a flying fuck whether or not her parents called. I was in no way obligated to create extra seats in my class for anyone, even spoiled business students who spent a semester binge drinking and fucking Italian guys.

I finished pulling together my notes and looking over the syllabus and in-class assignment I'd planned as a dozen or more students filed in, chattering and making the chairs squeak as they settled themselves at their desks. This was a small classroom with thirty or so of the old-fashioned desks with the tops on hinges. Students hated them because they were barely big enough for a notebook, let alone a laptop, which many of them brought to take notes.

After stepping over to the podium, I checked the clock on the instructor station computer. It was one minute past nine. Time to get started. I scanned the rows of desks and mustered a smile.

"Good morning! I'm Dr. Zara Ames."

And that was when I saw him. Last row. He stuck out like a sore thumb because he was much older than the barely legal students surrounding him. He had thick hair that was a little more pepper than salt and a layer of steel and silver stubble outlining his square jaw. His blue-green eyes haunted me, not looking much different than they had so many years before. *How many years? Twenty?*

No. It couldn't be him. My heart raced as I scrambled to convince myself there was just an uncanny resemblance between the man in the last row and someone I used to know long ago.

I glanced down at my roster. I hardly ever looked at it before class began. Having a running tally of seats taken on the course management system rendered looking at individual names unnecessary. My lungs squeezed in my chest as my eyes ran over thirty student names, and there his was in black and white:

Shea Michael Hunt.

My high school bully was sitting in my college class.

Shea

I probably missed the first two minutes of whatever this English professor was droning on about while I finished a text conversation with my daughter. I hardly ever heard from her now that she was in California, and there was such a big time difference. Plus, I was working this shitty part-time security gig, and the hours were killing me. I still wasn't sure how I was going to work, take classes, handle all the other things on my plate—and still find time to sleep and eat.

"So, what I need you to do now is to pair up with someone nearby. You're going to brainstorm a topic," the professor said. "It should be a controversial issue of some sort. You are going to take one side of it, and your partner will take the other. Then you're going to each write a paragraph expressing your views and exchange papers. You'll need to respond to their paragraph with one of your own, rebutting your partner's opinion. You'll have twenty minutes to complete this assignment. I want you to get used to thinking on your feet and getting the words to flow—"

I zoned out as I glanced around the room at potential partners. It looked like my fellow classmates were doing the same, which meant no one was listening to the professor. She had one of those soothing low-pitched voices, like you might hear in a commercial for a prescription drug. "Side effects include nausea, diarrhea, constipation..."

I glanced up when she shouted in a stern voice, "I'm not finished yet."

Her low-pitched voice had risen a whole octave, and her jaw was clenched so tight, it looked like it might shatter. That was when I first noticed her.

Her slightly wavy dark brown hair fell to her chin,

contrasting with her creamy, pale complexion and peach-toned cheeks. I couldn't tell what color her eyes were from the back row, but they were full of fire. Even from clear across the room, I could feel the heat they radiated.

But it was her curvy figure that really drew my attention. She wore a wrap dress that tied around the waist, and her ample hips and large breasts were impossible to ignore. Her thick legs ended in shiny black heels, and her fingers were long and elegant as they gripped her hips in apparent frustration.

She finished giving our assignment once she had everyone's attention. "I won't hesitate to keep you past the end of class if you continue to waste my time."

Wow, she's a hard ass, isn't she? I'd had a couple of tough professors in my first go-around in college, only to drop out after spending more time at frat parties than in the library studying. But none of my professors looked like her. Maybe I would have tried harder if they did!

I glanced down at the syllabus I'd pulled up on my laptop. I just wanted to see her name—that way I'd know what to call her later tonight when I jerked off thinking about those mouthwatering curves.

My eyes nearly popped out of my head when I read, "Zara Ames, PhD."

I'd only ever known one person named Zara in my entire life, and that was in high school.

Surely this wasn't the same Zara.

That Zara was mousy, insecure, and quite a nerd, with dark brown hair and thick glasses. That Zara was chubby and klutzy and always had her nose buried in a book. Though she was pretty for a shy, nerdy girl—and I might have even had a slight secret crush on her—this professor was a curvy goddess. Bold, full of herself—clearly on a power trip.

I had to know if it was the same Zara. But it couldn't be, right?

* * *

I sat at my desk, fiddling with my phone until every last student had filed out of the room. Dr. Ames was standing behind the lectern doing something on the computer, but she'd turned the projector off, so whatever was capturing her attention was private. Her dark brows arched as she appeared to read something, her eyes bouncing over the text, and she didn't even look up when I walked to the podium and stood.

I breathed in a whiff of her perfume—a deep, dark mysterious scent of exotic flowers and possibly vanilla. Like everything else about her, it was sophisticated and edgy. I was still having trouble reconciling this Zara with the Zara I knew twenty-five years ago.

And yes, I did the math. Next year we'd be forty-three, and we'd be having our quarter-of-a-century high school reunion. Not that I'd go. I never went. But it didn't change the length of time that had passed since graduation.

Math, I could do. English...English was another story. I'd never been good at writing papers or at grammar.

Her eyes popped up from the screen and landed on me. She appeared to suck in a deep breath, and her whole body went rigid at the sight of me. *Recognition, perhaps?*

"May I help you?" she asked in that smooth, even voice. From our class period, I learned she had two voices: the regular low-pitched soothing one and raging bitch mode.

"Oh, hi. I haven't taken English since my first semester of college twenty-some years ago," I admitted.

Did I really just fucking say that? What kind of idiot tells his professor that?

I searched her face for signs she knew who I was.

Maybe it was better if she didn't. Come to think of it, I wasn't particularly nice to her back then, despite having a crush on her—or maybe *because* I had a crush on her. But maybe she'd forgotten me completely. Hopefully.

Yes. That would be better.

"Okay?" was all she said in response, those eyebrows arching again.

"I just wanted you to know," I stated. *Like a total dumbass.*

"Well, thanks for the heads up." It looked like she tried to suppress a tiny smirk before her eyes shifted back to the computer screen. They were a warm brown, like melting chocolate. And still on fire.

"Um, sure. No problem," I muttered before stepping past her.

Once I got in the hall, I realized my heart was thundering inside my chest.

Something about her really made me nervous. But, yeah, it was definitely Zara Fowler. She definitely wasn't a shy nerd anymore.

And if she remembered who I was, there was a good chance I wasn't going to pass this class.

Two

Zara

I WATCHED Shea Hunt make his way out of my classroom with a lump in my throat the size of Texas. *What in the actual fuck is he doing in my class? And did he even recognize me?*

He didn't say so. Maybe he didn't. Hopefully he didn't. *That* was *him, wasn't it?*

When all my classes were done for the day, I rushed home, scrambled into the house and nearly tripped over the cat when he tried to weave his way between my legs on the way to the giant bookcase in my living room. Yes, he just wanted to be greeted and then properly fed, but I had something more urgent on my mind: looking up Shea Hunt.

It had been almost twenty-five years. Maybe I was misremembering what he looked like?

No, those eyes. Those eyes were the same. That piercing

blue-green, like knives slicing right through you. I flipped through the pages of my senior yearbook, heading straight to the section with our full-color senior poses, where all the girls were wearing formal dresses, and the boys were wearing tuxes.

There he was. His hair was a sandy brown, a little long and spiky on top. His face was thinner, his nose a little less distinguished. He was handsome in a jock kind of way. His mouth was curled in that menacing smirk that was nearly as memorable as his stabbing turquoise stare.

It was him. There was no doubt.

Shea Michael Hunt.

My finger slid over the smooth page as a tear stung at the corner of my eyes. I'd suffered—not at his hands. No, he never touched me. It was his mouth that hurt me. The things he said about me, *to me*. The arrows he shot right into my heart.

One time...

My heart broke all over again as the memory crashed down upon me before I had a chance to stop it. I was powerless when it consumed me, seizing my mind and holding me in its sharp talons. In seconds, I was transported back to high school, the shy, nerdy, overweight girl clutching my stack of textbooks to my chest as Shea Hunt, the star of the high school basketball team, stopped in front of my locker. He was flanked by his all-star jock posse.

"Hey, you goin' to the homecoming dance?" He looked me up and down with that dirty, demeaning stare of his.

My throat closed up, my lungs bucking for air. In lieu of words, I shook my head.

Then he said something I could scarcely believe—words I never fathomed would come out of his mouth:

"Do you wanna go to the dance with me?"

His posse gathered around him, all of them leering at me, waiting on pins and needles for my mouth to open. His mouth twisted up into that damn smirk as his eyes missile-locked on me.

My heartbeat rocketed up to a million beats per minute; my lungs fought for air, and my spine prickled like I'd backed up against barbed wire. My lips, tongue, none of it was working. I just stared at him.

He was joking, right?

Then his smirk softened into something that almost looked warm, caring. His eyes seemed to twinkle as he blinked, awaiting my answer. "Pretty please?" he sweetened the deal.

"Uh..." Finally, I uttered a sound. It was as difficult to produce as turning a nugget of lead to gold.

"C'mon, Zara," he begged.

"Uh, okay..." More alchemy.

I waited for him to smile in confirmation, but instead he turned around to the six-foot-seven dude who was our basketball team's center. Growing up in central Indiana, that made him a god.

"You owe me fifty bucks!" Shea exclaimed. "I asked her!"

The entire group huddled around us burst into laughter, all snickering at how the awkward nerdy fat girl had actually believed the basketball star wanted to take her to the homecoming dance.

I froze in place, trapped against the lockers. I had to stand there and take their ridicule, their taunts.

He scoffed, "Yeah, right. Like I'd actually take a fat girl to the dance!"

Their cruel laughter still echoed in my mind twenty-five years later.

It still haunted me to this day. But if I hadn't pulled myself up by the bootstraps and learned to love every single fucking inch of myself—despite what those motherfucking bullies did to me—then I would have let Shea Hunt be in charge of how I saw myself.

Thank FUCK I didn't let him win.

Now, I had a chance to shape Shea Hunt's future, just like he tried to shape mine. I had a chance to fuck with his self-esteem, with his identity. With his future.

You had better believe I didn't come this fucking far to let a little fucking asshole like Shea Hunt pass my class—not unless he absolutely one hundred percent deserved to.

* * *

A few hours later, I picked up the yearbook to put it back on the shelf, where I hoped the memories of the way Shea Hunt tortured me would stay. A slip of paper fell out, and as soon as I saw it, my heart jumped off a cliff.

My vision blurred as I read the first poem I ever wrote. The poem that made me a poet.

> I wish you could see me the way
> I see you
> You're an eclipse
> Obscuring my moon
> No matter how full I am
> You're always fuller
> My light snuffed out
> By your sun
> I wish you could see me the way
> I see you

And maybe you'd
Let me shine

Shea

"Hey, I'm home." I closed the door to the garage quietly behind me as I stepped into the kitchen. "Did Judy leave?"

No answer. Not that I was expecting one.

I put the bag of groceries on the counter and set the oven to 400 degrees. I did buy some ingredients to make a nice dinner, but I was exhausted from class and shopping, and I needed to leave at nine for my job. So tonight was another frozen pizza night. Not that anyone would care. Hopefully tomorrow I'd feel like making the shrimp pasta dish I bought groceries for.

"Long day," I said as I unwrapped the pizza and got it ready for the oven. "Had my first English class today, plus the two business classes I told you about. English is gonna be really tough."

I washed my hands and grabbed a bag of salad from the fridge. After pouring it into a bowl, I added some onions, tomatoes, and green peppers, chopping them carefully on a wooden cutting board before tossing them in with the lettuce. If I was going to eat pizza, I might as well have something healthy to go with it. Not like I was gonna see the inside of a gym anytime soon, not now that classes had started.

"Hey, do you have any idea where my high school yearbook is?" I called out into the empty space, my own voice ringing between my ears. "I wanna look up this professor. I'm pretty sure she's someone I went to high school with."

No answer. Not that I was expecting one.

I set the salad aside and went into the living room, past the figure in the armchair covered with a knitted afghan. After flipping the light on, I went to the coat closet near the front door we never used. Inside was an old, dilapidated cardboard box full of my high school memories. My letter jacket was in there, along with my cap from graduation. The remains of my prom boutonnière were flaking away on top of a neat stack of programs for basketball games and other events. On the bottom was my senior year high school yearbook, a solid tome with a faux leather binding and the year of my graduation stamped in gold.

I pulled it out, breathing in that old book smell, and flipped the thick, glossy pages to the center, where the senior pictures were displayed. I scanned each row until my eyes landed on Zara Fowler.

Same pale, creamy skin and dark hair, though it was longer back then. She wore thick glasses and had chubby cheeks. Her smile, though. It was the same. The same full lips and nice teeth, the kind that never needed braces, just naturally perfect and white. I noticed that today—they looked as nice as ever.

Her face had matured. She was still full-figured, but she'd grown into her hourglass shape. Her facial features were more defined, and those eyes, not hiding behind glasses any longer, they were so striking, so penetrating, a dark amber like the blackest part of a flame.

She was a nerd in high school, and apparently, she still was. She was a professor. She went by Dr. Ames. I assumed that meant she was married. Her being an academic wasn't surprising in the least. She always had her nose buried in a book.

My friends and I gave her a hard time.

But secretly, I thought she was pretty. And smart. She was my lab partner in bio freshman year. We dissected a frog together. I'd never forget how brave she was slicing into that thing. She wasn't the least bit fazed.

I had a bit of a crush on her, but there was no way I could admit it to my friends. They would have given me hell. So I might have joined in a little harmless ribbing.

Doesn't look like it held her back...

"Yeah," I shared with the figure sitting silently, stoically in the recliner, "it's definitely her. Zara Fowler. Haven't thought about her in almost twenty-five years."

I heaved a sigh as I put the yearbook back down in the box and rose to face the shadowed figure. "Do you think you'll feel like eating something tonight?"

No answer. Not that I was expecting one.

"I'm making a pizza. You can have some if you want."

"Michael, did you get the laundry detergent from the store like I asked?" came a soft, rambling voice. There wasn't much inflection, just words mumbled from rote memory. "I've gotta make some cookies for the bake sale. Michael, can you leave the oven on?"

I fell to my knees in front of the recliner and put my head on her lap. "I can leave the oven on, but I'm not Michael. I'm Shea. Don't you remember me?"

"The Oldsmobile needs an oil change. Can you take it into the shop on Friday?" She began to rock back and forth, clutching the afghan in her gnarled, age-spotted hands. "Michael, where's Caroline? Can you get her for me? I want to show her the dress I bought for her First Communion."

I shook my head. I hated it when she did this. It was

better when she was just silent. I could never predict when she would have an outburst, either.

She rambled on, "Caroline! C'mon in here and let me see how you look. Do I need to take it in? Let me get my pin cushion."

I closed my eyes and tried to imagine having her whole again. Having her healed. It would never happen. She would continue to decline.

One day she wouldn't even remember Michael or Caroline. I should feel grateful she remembered them, but it was a slap in the face that my father and sister had been dead for decades, and she remembered them but not me, her only son who had taken care of her for years. Not to mention the fact that my father was a total asshole. By the way she talked about him, you'd think he was a fucking saint.

But fuck, Alzheimer's is a bitch.

I must have sat there longer than I thought because the oven timer beeping snapped me out of my daze. "I'm gonna go get the pizza, Mom. Do you want any?"

She waved her hand at me. Sometimes she didn't eat for days. She did drink though. I got her to drink those protein shakes for older people. I'd make her one of those while the pizza was cooling.

I headed back into the kitchen and turned off the beeping timer.

"Don't set off the smoke alarm, Michael!" my mother called from the living room.

Sighing, I slid the pizza out of the oven. I had an hour to eat this and get ready for work. Hopefully Judy would be back by then to get my mother ready for bed. I wasn't sure how I would be able to take care of her without the neighbor, who was a nurse. I was able to pay her a little, but now that I'd lost my job and blown through my savings, I didn't know how much longer I could keep up the arrangement. This part-time security job I did at night didn't pay shit.

I needed to finish my degree and start my dream job ASAP. I only hoped the offer would still be there when I finally managed to graduate.

Three

Zara

MY LUNGS SQUEEZED in my chest, like I couldn't get enough oxygen as I knocked on the frame of my department chair's door. Every time I had to talk to him, a nauseated feeling churned in the pit of my stomach.

He waved me in, and I went to stand in front of his desk like a child sent to the principal's office. "You can have a seat," he said without looking up from the large binder on his desk.

It was my tenure binder; I just knew it. My jaw clenched even tighter as I scooted out the chair and settled myself in it, arranging my skirt so none of my thigh showed.

I always tried to dress professionally, but my curvy figure had a habit of making the most innocuous outfit look salacious. Other professors could wear a fitted sweater and a pencil skirt and look demure. I looked like the love child of Dolly Parton and The Rock or something. I had height, a large frame, and big hips and boobs to match.

"You wanted to see me?" I prompted him when it appeared he was simply going to ignore me. I only had a finite amount of time between classes, so I would appreciate it if he cut to the chase. But I knew better than to snap at him when he had my tenure file on his desk. I had to play nice, or he'd deny my tenure. He'd done it before to other professors he didn't like.

Alan Palmer was a small, petty man, and he seemed rather intent on making my teaching career a living hell.

"Yes, thank you for taking time out of your busy schedule to drop by." He lifted his beady gray eyes over his glasses and pinned them on me.

"You're welcome. Do you mind telling me why you asked to see me?" I didn't mean to sound so...biting...but this man made my skin crawl.

"So I've been looking through your dossier. I appreciate that you wanted me to review it before you turned it in to your tenure and promotion committee. I know you were looking for some feedback to strengthen your case."

"Yes?" I schooled my features to remain in a neutral state, but it was taking every ounce of restraint I had.

"Do you have anything else you can include for your publishing section?" He leaned in, lacing his fingers together on the surface of his desk. "The book of poetry, while I'm sure it's perfectly charming, isn't a very rigorously refereed publication. Who was the publisher again?"

I rattled off the name of the academic press that published my first volume of poems last year. The editor seemed hopeful they would be interested in a second volume in another year or two.

"Exactly," he bit back. "I rest my case." His chest rose as

he sucked in a deep breath, one of consternation. "I just don't want to see your dossier rejected because of a weak publication record. Have you co-authored any papers? Presented at any major conferences? You may not have realized that even co-authored journal articles and presentations count toward your publication criteria."

My heart sank. Was he warning me my tenure bid was going to be rejected? What would I do if I failed to make tenure? They would maybe keep me on as a lecturer... I wasn't sure. I'd have to consult my contract. The thought of not making it had never seriously occurred to me.

"I take that as a no?"

My brain was scrambling for something, anything, that might work. "Oh, well, I did present at a literacy conference two years ago," I shared. "Not MLA or one of the other language ones. It was an education conference, but it was national. It was in San Diego. I can get you the abstract."

"You should have put that in here." He shoved the binder toward me. It already contained my curriculum vitae, all of my smaller publications, all the curriculum innovations I'd come up with in the past few years, all the committee work I'd done, and letters of recommendation from anyone and everyone up to and including God. *Well, that last one might be a slight exaggeration...*

"I can update it. Thank you for pointing out the oversight. And I will see if I have done anything else that might be of interest to the committee."

"See that you have that back in my hands by tomorrow," he sneered. "The committee's first meeting is Friday morning, and I'd hate for your dossier to be incomplete..."

He let the words trail off like it was a warning as to what might happen if my binder was missing the minutest detail. As though the committee could possibly review the entire thing in one meeting. No, some secretary would kill a forest full of trees making a copy for all five committee members. Why it couldn't be done digitally was beyond me. That was truly the worst part of academia...the *we've always done it this way, so we will do it that way until time itself ends.*

"Thanks," I said, the one syllable clipped and curt as I stood up and smoothed down my skirt over my ample thighs. As I left his office, I felt his stare searing into my backside.

Alan Palmer was a small, petty man. And a creepy one too.

* * *

I suffered through my next class—or I should say, my students did—then headed back to my own office. It only took one essay from my intensive writing class to nauseate me, destroying my appetite for lunch. They were pitiful.

They're just drafts, Zara, I told myself. *And we're only two weeks into the semester.* I wore out my hand writing notes in the margins and making proofreader marks they likely wouldn't even understand. I'd have to go over those in class tomorrow. I needed to hand them back ASAP; otherwise my whole schedule would be thrown off.

When I came to Shea Hunt's paper, I cringed. It was like he had no idea what a comma was, much less how to use one. His syntax was sloppy, his argumentation sorely lacking.

It was painfully obvious he spent high school goofing off—probably getting drunk and/or high and seeing how many girls he could bed. He certainly wasn't learning how to write a proper essay.

All those years he bullied me and made my life a living

hell were going to come back to bite him in the ass. I finally, finally had a chance to teach him a lesson.

I couldn't fucking wait to bleed red ink all over this pathetic excuse for a paper.

Shea

Professor Hottie was looking amazing in her plaid skirt, tights that showed off her shapely calves, and a pair of heels. She was like a fine wine—only growing richer and more luscious with age. Okay, so it was a clichéd compliment, but I was working on about four hours of sleep. *You really can't expect much better than that.*

When she walked by my desk and slapped down the graded version of the essay I'd turned in last week, she didn't even make eye contact. I couldn't tell if she didn't recognize or remember me, or if she was still mad at me over the harmless ribbing I did in high school.

I didn't think I looked that different—sure, there were a few wrinkles around my eyes, and I had a bit more salt in my hair—but everyone from my past always assured me I hadn't aged a day since we were kids.

Sucking in an anxious breath, I turned the essay over to see her feedback. The entire class was doing the same. She said she'd give us five minutes to read the feedback before she addressed us. The way she said it, her tone was filled with defeat. And with as feisty as she'd been during our other class sessions, I didn't think that boded well for our grades.

Sure enough, I looked over the comments—there was as

much red ink on the paper as there was white space—and my heart sank lower and lower. She called my argument "weak and nonsensical." There were all sorts of things circled. Arrows going every which way. I almost needed a decoder to decipher some of the marks.

As I made it to the last page of the four-page essay, she cleared her throat, prompting everyone to lift their eyes to the front of the room and place them right on her. "Put down your papers," she instructed. "I want your full attention."

There was a bit of murmuring at that.

"I will not tell you again," she repeated, her voice lower and flatter than before, definitely an edge of frustration to it.

That garnered silence, all of us focused on her and her alone.

She let out a long sigh as she prepared to speak. And then she let loose: "Look, you all graduated from high school, right?"

Everyone nodded, and there was a bit of snickering.

"I am assuming you wrote at least a few papers in high school. And then you had to take a basic comp class and a literature class before taking this one, so even if you haven't had to write papers for any of your other classes, I'm sure you had to write some research papers for those prerequisites."

Everyone stared at her.

"Look, MLA citation and formatting is not just a suggestion. It's required. When I say you need three sources, that's at a bare minimum. When I say you need to make a coherent argument with a solid conclusion, that's not negotiable. Am I making myself clear?"

There were a few nods, and when I glanced around, I saw a scowl or two.

"I don't sugarcoat things," she continued. "You may have read on Rate My Professor Dot Com that I'm a hard ass. Well, I hate to be the one to shout, but you don't learn how to write without two things: one is lots and lots of practice, and the other is constructive feedback. You are going to get both in this class.

"Now, this is our starting point. I expect you to take my feedback and improve your drafts before you submit the final versions to me next week. In the meantime, if you feel you need extra help, I recommend visiting the Writing Center here on campus. They will be more than happy to help you with the mechanics of your papers. If you need help finding sources, the librarians at the reference desk in the main library would be ecstatic to help you. Help is readily available. There's really no excuse for not learning in this class, because you have resources at your disposal. But you can't be lazy asses who don't actually put forth some effort if you want to pass. Am I clear?"

Slow nods all around.

"I'm giving you the rest of our class period today to get a jump start on your revisions. You can come see me during my office hours if you have any questions."

Everyone started to file out, but my eyes were still glued to Dr. Ames. It was almost hard for me to see the shy, insecure girl I knew in high school when I looked at her, but I knew she was in there. Maybe I could appeal to that girl when I asked her for help, because if she didn't take pity on me, I was going to flunk this class. And it wouldn't be because I was a "lazy ass" or didn't want to put forth effort, but because I was working my ass off and trying to take care of my mother.

And if I flunked this class, I couldn't get into business school, which meant I couldn't get a business degree, which meant I couldn't get the job I'd basically been promised. I'd fucked up so many times, in so many ways, and I finally had a chance to make something of myself. To redeem myself from all the shitty things I'd done or let happen through the years.

It's like every damn thing in my life hinges on this class.

Who would have thought my future would rest in the hands of Zara Fowler?

My best bet? Pour on the trademark Shea Hunt charm and pretend like we'd never met. I wouldn't want her bad memories of me from high school to color her evaluation of my work. So far, it didn't seem like she recognized me, so I would just assume she hadn't...and wouldn't. I definitely wasn't going to bring it up—and hopefully she wouldn't either.

Squaring my shoulders, I ambled up to her desk, tossing my backpack on top of it like I was claiming the space for myself. "Hi..." The single word floated out of my mouth.

She looked up from her instructor station, her dark eyes full of annoyance as they met mine. But she quickly cleared her throat again, as I noticed she had a bad habit of doing, and plastered a smile on her beautiful face. "Hi, sorry. I was just reading an email."

"I didn't mean to interrupt you," I offered. "Listen, I wanted to talk to you about my paper." I tossed it face up on the table next to my backpack, the sea of red marks glaring at us.

She picked it up, her eyes dancing over the words like she needed a refresher on who I was. *She really doesn't remember me. Interesting.* I was one of the most popular kids in school, and we did have a few interactions. She was in my bio class. As a matter of fact, we were lab partners freshman year.

"Yes, Mr. Hunt, I remember your essay." She tried to say it neutrally, but her tone betrayed her disgust at my butchering of the English language.

"So...I'm not asking you for special favors. I don't want you to think that." I waited for her eyes to lift from the paper and return to mine. I wanted her to see my sincerity. What was really just one rung above begging.

"What *are* you asking for?" she fired back, her lips trembling ever so slightly like she was trying not to smile.

"I work full-time," I stretched the truth, "and I have this plus a couple other classes, so I don't have a lot of free time. The Writing Center's hours conflict with my schedule."

"I see."

Just those two words, barely a shift in her expression.

"So...when do you have time to work on your projects, Mr. Hunt?" She tapped her long nails on the desk beside her instructor station.

"Honestly, the only time I have outside of class is dinnertime until about eight PM and on the weekends. Maybe very early in the morning when I get off work, but obviously the Writing Center isn't open then."

"Right."

She continued to look at me. I wasn't sure what she expected me to say or do next, so I just kept rambling, hoping my charm would persuade her to help me. "I really need to pass this class. I'm trying to get into business school, and this is the one class I need."

"I see."

Her answers were so short, so curt. But I still didn't see recognition flashing in her eyes. I was pretty sure she was just a "hard ass," like the Rate My Professor site said. I didn't have a choice though—this was the only section of the intensive writing course that fit into my crazy schedule.

Her nostrils flared ever so slightly. "Can you meet tonight?"

I tried to suppress a grin. "Yes, ma'am. What time is good for you?"

Moments later, I was strutting down the hall, that grin I'd suppressed earlier forcing its way across my face.

Four

Zara

FOR SOME INEXPLICABLE REASON, I decided to go home after my last class and take a shower before meeting Shea Hunt back in my office at seven to go over his paper. I couldn't get those teal-blue eyes and sexy grin out of my mind.

For some reason, this man—the bane of my existence in high school—was about a hundred times hotter now that he was in his early forties. Not that he wasn't hot in high school. On the contrary, he was widely considered the cutest boy in our class, plus he was the star player on our basketball team, which is basically divine status in Indiana.

But now... *Damn.* I didn't know if it was the silver coming in around the edges of his otherwise brown hair or the faint dimples that slightly popped out in his facial scruff when I finally agreed to meet with him. Or maybe it was his smirky grin, his broad shoulders, thick arms, or his mouth-watering backside.

It would be a lot easier to exact revenge on this asshole if he wasn't so fucking hot.

I looked in the mirror as I held up a couple of different outfit choices. *Why are you obsessing about this? You're having a meeting. A professor-student meeting. Nothing inappropriate can happen. You're going to put him through his paces and make him work his ass off to pass this class.*

And if he doesn't work his ass off? I will happily flunk him. No questions asked.

I went with a classic V-neck sweater—work-appropriate, but at certain angles you got the barest hint of cleavage. And jeans. Because it was after hours and why not? Besides I had a pair that made my voluptuous ass look like a juicy peach. Or at least that was what some creepy dude called out to me in the parking lot at the grocery store the other day when I was pushing my cart to my Nissan SUV.

Unlocking my office door, I reminded myself for the four hundredth time that tonight was about laying out what was expected in my class and letting Mr. Hunt know he must improve his writing technique considerably to earn a passing grade. And I vowed not to give him any indication that I remembered him from high school.

I couldn't.

If I did, I was afraid I would break down in front of him.

Some of the things he said to me back then echoed in my memory for years. I'd worked so fucking hard to destroy those demons that whispered horribly cruel things to me about my body, about my worth in this world.

But he didn't break me. Maybe I was stronger because

of him. Maybe I had learned to love myself and my body *because* of him, *because of what he put me through.*

Maybe I should thank him.

Ha! Like that's ever going to happen.

It didn't matter. It was crazy to think he could be interested in me now. He ridiculed me back then, acted like I could never attract a boyfriend. I was even curvier now than back in high school, so unless his tastes had matured...

Gah! It doesn't matter! We are here to work. Period.

I perched at my desk, awaiting his arrival. If he was even a minute late... But two minutes till seven, three sharp raps sounded on my office door.

"Come in," I called out as evenly as I could.

The door handle twisted, and his handsome face appeared, that sheepish dimpled grin spreading across his cheeks once more. "Thanks again for agreeing to meet."

"Of course." I kept my tone curt, mannerisms stiff as I pointed to the chair across from me. We were separated by the three-foot-wide expanse of my desk. I hoped it would be enough of a buffer, because sitting here, locking stares with the boy who'd teased me relentlessly in high school, then grew up to be hotter than a raging inferno—well, I didn't know whether I would rather slap his face or jump his bones.

You're going to flunk his ass, Zara. And you're going to enjoy the hell out of doing so.

He settled himself in the chair and withdrew the paper, all sliced up and bleeding with red ink, from his backpack. "Well, here it is. Sorry I'm so out of practice writing. I've been doing computer programming for the last two decades..."

"Computer programming," I repeated. That didn't sound like the Shea Hunt I remembered from high school.

That required patience, tenacity—it was a lonely, isolating job. I imagined him in some dank cubicle, lines of code scrolling by on his computer monitor as he typed away on his keyboard. I couldn't think of anything more soul-sucking than that.

He nodded. "Yeah. I always liked computers, and my basketball coach from high school owned a computer store. I worked there in the summers and picked up some stuff from clients there. Went to work for one when I dropped out of college."

He said "basketball coach from high school" like I wouldn't know he was talking about Coach Finch. Did he really not remember me either? Well, I did look different from high school. Different hair. No glasses. New last name.

"I see. Why did you leave that job?" I asked, though I knew we should start focusing on his paper. *Curiosity killed the cat and all that...*

"It's a long story. Um...not a very flattering one." He chuckled a little...humorlessly...as he looked down at the surface of the desk. I sensed he was embarrassed he had just shared that with me. What was I supposed to surmise other than he was fired?

"So time for a career change?" I tried to lighten the mood, probably unsuccessfully. I felt the tension stirring between us like there was a third person in the room. It seemed to go beyond normal professor-student tension. It seemed even worse than former-high-school-bully-and-victim-reconnect-in-strange-new-power-dynamic-twenty-five-years-later...

Was it...sexual tension?

"Yeah." That wicked smile stretched his lips before his tongue darted out to lick the top one ever so briefly, like it was a bad habit he couldn't control. Then it disappeared as he sucked in a deep breath and let it out again. "Sorry I'm nervous; I…" His eyes met mine square on for the first time, and an electric jolt buzzed down my spine.

"It's okay. Professors can be intimidating, but we're just regular people," I joked, still trying to keep it light. "I mean, we do wield a lot of power, but—"

He seemed to understand I was joking, and his dimples returned. "I want to get into business school and finish my degree. I've been preliminarily offered a job that will be opening around the time I'll graduate. It's with a nonprofit, so—"

"Communication skills are very important in that field," I interjected, steering this conversation back to his paper. I had to, or we'd be here forever. "You will need strong writing skills, and that's why we're here, right?"

"I believe so." There was that lip-lick again, and I got a sense he could have ulterior motives.

He wouldn't seduce me to get a better grade in the class, would he?

"Well, there are several things you can work on that will give you a leg up, okay?" I pointed to his paper. "Do you want to jot down some notes?"

He chuckled as he fumbled his pen in his fingers, and all I could think of was the fact that, in high school, he was known for his smooth passing, shooting, and ball-handling abilities. He was the star of the basketball team for a reason: he had mad skills and ice in his veins when it came to hitting tough shots. But all these years later, he couldn't even hold on to his pen. I seemed to make him nervous.

"Sorry, I—" He shook his head as his eyes darted down to his notebook and then back up again. "I just really want to learn the right way to do this."

For some reason, it didn't seem like he was really talking about writing all of the sudden, not when there was a persistent heat smoldering in his gaze. I sucked in a deep breath and conjured up images of him from high school, all those times he said cruel, hateful things to me.

Was he really interested in learning how to improve his writing, or did he want something else...?

I just couldn't shake the way his gaze drilled into me as I explained what I wanted from him. I was trying so hard to keep it professional, and he issued me a challenge every time his tongue darted out to lick his lips.

We worked together for the next forty minutes, me going through his paper section by section to detail what he needed to improve in his next draft. He was receptive, humble, and most surprisingly—considering the ego he had in high school—grateful.

"Would it be okay if I came back later this week to show you what I've got so far? To see if it's more to your liking?" His brow rose as he awaited my answer, hope dancing in those turquoise eyes.

Again, I wasn't entirely sure he was talking about writing.

But what plans could he possibly interrupt? Hanging out at home with my cat and papers to grade?

"Um, sure, I guess that'll be okay," I decided before I could overanalyze too much.

A smile spread across his face, reaching clear to his eyes. "Thanks again, Dr. Ames. I can't tell you how much this means to me." He gathered up his things and stuffed them in his backpack. "I'll see you in class."

Watching him walk out, I shook my head. It was going to be a hell of a lot harder to flunk him if he was going to be so charming and grateful for my help. How could I keep hating him when he seemed like he'd turned out to be a nice person?

Unless it was all a ploy to get in my pants. I still hadn't ruled that out.

This is your high school bully, I reminded myself. *The boy who made you cry and write sappy poetry.*

He doesn't deserve your mercy.

Shea

Zara dropped her hard-ass act in her office tonight. I couldn't get over how down-to-earth she was. And gracious. I had turned in a steaming pile of shit, but she never made me feel like a failure. She somehow found nice ways to tell me all the many, many ways I'd fucked up my paper.

There was absolutely no way she knew who I was. There was no way she could treat me so nicely if she remembered what an ass I was in high school.

If I did pass this class, it would only be because Zara Fowler Ames was a class act.

By the way... I still wanted to fuck her.

I wanted to fuck her even more than I did before.

That was why I asked her to meet with me again. I was sure I could muddle my way through my notes and come up with something halfway decent for my second draft, but I just wanted to see her again. Be alone with her again.

"You okay, Mom?" I asked as I finished getting dressed for school. I'd rushed home to make sure Mom was fed and ready for Judy to come before I headed in for my shift.

I wasn't expecting an answer. And I didn't get one.

Maybe I shouldn't get so hung up on the fact that Zara didn't recognize me from high school.

My own mother didn't recognize me, and she fucking gave birth to me.

Five

Shea

IT WAS our second meeting in her office, and this woman was driving me absolutely mad. Why was it so difficult to concentrate on my paper when I was sitting this close to her? Her perfume was all exotic florals and a deep, erotic vanilla. It made my cock leap to attention, rendering me tongue-tied. It didn't help that I'd jerked off thinking about her a half-dozen times since our last meeting.

She asked if we were here to work on my writing...and I said, "I believe so."

As sincerely as I wanted to improve my writing skills, I just as sincerely wanted to lift her out of that chair, toss her up on her desk, spread her legs and dive in between her thighs. I needed to know if her floral scent was stronger at her center, and if she tasted as good as she smelled.

I'm gonna predict the answer to that is hell yes!

"Tonight let's talk a little more about your sources,

okay? Those are the foundation of your argument," she began. When she turned back to her computer and started to type, I noticed how long and elegant her fingers looked as they struck the keys. She wore a ring on her right ring finger. It looked like an emerald surrounded by diamonds. A family heirloom perhaps? Nothing on her left hand. She had a different last name, but no wedding rings.

I ached to move closer. "I'm having trouble seeing your screen. Do you mind if I move my chair?"

She didn't look at me, just answered, "Sure, no problem."

I brought my chair around next to her, and now I was close enough to touch her. The jeans she wore clung to her thick thighs, and I was still envisioning them wrapped around my head. *Concentrate on the screen, man*, I chided myself.

"This is one of the library databases. So I put in some keywords for your topic. What you want to do is look for the ones in academic journals—you know, scholarly sources. Nothing from a newspaper or magazine."

"Alright..."

She pointed to the screen. "This one looks good, and this study was published only a year ago. It's recent and relevant."

I leaned toward the desk to get a better look at the screen and breathed in her scent again. My cock stiffened even more. Not only could I smell her, but I could sense her heat. She was angled away from me toward the computer. The graceful curve of her neck and the scalloped edge of her earlobe called to me. I wanted to sink my teeth right into that spot where her neck met her shoulder, then trail kisses up to her ear, making her shiver with need.

Fuck! Why couldn't I stay focused tonight?

She turned to look at me then, and she must have caught the lustful look in my eye because her breath hitched. As she shifted in her chair, I saw the slightest tremble of her hand as it gripped the mouse. She had figured it out. That I was staring at her. That I wanted her.

The ball was in her court...

Now what would our professor do?

Zara

God, did he really just look at me like that? Like he wanted to claim me right here on this desk, throw me down on the surface, strip me down nude and have his way with me?

I scrambled for something to say because his gaze was drilling into me, insistent and urgent. A shudder racked my body as I tried to coax my lungs into working properly again.

His eyes were fucking me. His lips were begging to explore. His broad, manly hands looked like they would give anything to stroke down my curves. The bulge in his pants was completely unmistakable.

Now it was clear: he wasn't just trying to seduce me to improve his grade, to pass my class. He wanted me. And he wanted me now.

He didn't remember who I was, and he had apparently developed a penchant for more full-figured women over the skinny cheerleader types he dated in high school. *Good for him...that's great. Just great.*

Because I hadn't had sex in six months, and my entire body was aching to be filled. Those smoldering eyes were too much to take. Those thick hands were pleading for a chance to caress my curves... It wasn't fucking fair! Why did he have to be so goddamn sexy?

But I couldn't.

I couldn't fuck a student. I promised myself from the very beginning of my career that I wouldn't—not ever. Not to mention the simple, basic, undeniable fact—even if I deserved an Oscar for pretending otherwise—this was SHEA FUCKING HUNT, the boy who tortured me in high school.

"Zara," his voice was so deep, it was nothing more than a growl, "what's going on in that beautiful head of yours?" He cocked his own head to the side as a smile made that dimple pop out from his brown and silver scruff.

"I...uh...I'm so sorry. Where were we?" I tried to tear my gaze from him and return it to my keyboard, hoping some little voice inside me, preferably the professional one, would give me the right words to type, the right words to say. Would help me avoid this temptation that I had never experienced before.

It was easy not to get involved with a student when they were two decades younger than me. I hadn't had a student so close to my age since my very first year of teaching. Every year I had a birthday, but my students stayed the same age: late teens and early twenties. There weren't many nontraditional age students in my courses, and most of the ones I'd taught were either women or much older than Shea Hunt.

"I think you know exactly where we are." He reached out, so slowly, I could have easily stopped him if I wanted to, and stroked his thick finger down my cheek, raking in a shallow breath as he did so, like he was surprised at how soft my skin was.

I held my breath for a moment, my lungs feeling like

they were about to explode as the shock of his touch rocketed through me. A familiar tingle radiated throughout my core, and I knew without touching myself that my panties were soaked. When I shifted just a tiny bit in my chair, it was enough to confirm my suspicions.

"Mr. Hunt—"

"Please, call me Shea." His eyes never left mine as he trailed his fingertips down my cheek and chin until they went back to rest on his jeans, inches from the bulge in his pants, like he was trying to direct my attention right to it.

"Shea, I...I don't date students," I managed, thankful that professional voice inside me was able to rise above the raging hormones.

"Who said anything about dating?" he rasped. "I sense you want me just as much as I want you..."

I huffed out a breath, unable to argue with that. *But I must. I have to.*

He licked his lip and settled his piercing turquoise gaze on me. "I'll make you a deal..."

My eyebrows arched as I stared at him, waiting for him to enlighten me on this "deal." I thought, as the professor, I was the one who was supposed to be making deals—and the deal with him was that he was supposed to work his ass off to pass this class.

But maybe there was a better way to get back at him for all the bullying he did in high school?

Maybe I should give in to temptation and enjoy the irony of him fucking the very same girl he made fun of for being too fat.

A revenge fuck, if you will.

How poetic!

And poetry is my jam.

"What kind of deal?" I asked when it looked like he'd decided not to tell me. Now I was too curious.

He stood up, and I got a mouthwatering view of his entire body. Button-down shirt with sleeves rolled to the elbow, accentuating strong, muscular forearms. Trim waist and hips stacked upon thick thighs framing that delectable-looking bulge right beneath the fly of his jeans. I had a feeling if he turned around and gave me a view of his ass, I'd be a goner. I'd always had a thing for men with nice tight, round bums. As a poet, I could very easily compose an ode to that ass.

"I know I shouldn't...because you're my professor, and I really want to learn from you," he filled me in, that grin on his face turning increasingly sheepish.

"What do you want to learn?" I stood up and faced him.

"I want to learn how to write," he admitted. "I really do." He took a step closer to me, reached out, and took my hand. "May I?"

I wasn't sure what he was going to do with my hand, but I nodded anyway.

He wasn't gripping my hand that tightly; I could have slipped out of his grasp if I wanted to. But next thing I knew he was guiding my hand toward his crotch.

"This is what you're doing to me," he explained. "I know it's not your fault. Or your responsibility. But I'm having a terrible time concentrating on anything but how good you smell and how beautiful you are..."

I struggled to keep my eyes from bugging out of my head when I felt his cock flex through the thick fabric of his jeans. I was no expert on cock sizes, but if my paltry experience served me correctly, he was packing considerable heat.

When I said nothing, a shocked lump stuck in my

throat, he continued, "The deal I was thinking of was...and feel free to say no..."

"Go on," I directed him, finally finding my voice.

His dimple flashed before he explained, "If you're wet right now...you break the rules and let me take you right over your desk."

My heart rate soared as I fired back, "And if I'm not?"

His lips curled. "If you're not, I'll just get out of your hair and figure out this writing thing myself. Oh, and I'll go home and jerk off...because this boner's not going away without some help."

His candid admission struck me. I never expected this to happen when he asked me to help him with his paper tonight. "But that means you have to—"

"Touch you," he finished for me. "Yes, that is a risk you must be willing to take..." His eyebrows arched suggestively.

Oh. My. God. This guy was too much! Did he really think I was going to—

Before I could stop myself, I reached down and unfastened the fly on my jeans, then shimmied them down my hips, baring my thighs and my black lace panties. What the fuck was I doing?

Calling his bluff! He doesn't really have the balls to finger me right in my office, does he?

With a sultry look smoldering in his turquoise gaze, he stepped toward me. He showed me his finger, then popped it in his mouth. "Just a little moisture...I don't want to hurt you."

I held my breath as his finger approached, skirting the edge of my panties and slipping in close to my heat. *He'll stop at the last minute, right? Right before he touches me?*

He pulled me into his other arm and dropped his head

to my shoulder, breathing in the scent of my hair. "God-damn, Zara..."

A soft wince parted my lips when he stroked his finger down the seam of my entrance, searching for passage. "Fuck," I moaned as his finger easily slid inside me and explored for a moment, deep enough to reach my G-spot.

I realized he knew exactly what the fuck he was doing when he curled his finger and rubbed it against the swollen bunch of nerves, making my knees buckle and a hot, breathy sigh escape my lips. I couldn't believe he actually did it.

He pulled his finger out, leaving me longing for so much more, and brought it to eye level, examining it. "Zara..." was all he said, eyebrows arched.

The way he said my name was...pure sexual energy. And there was absolutely no way I could deny that his finger was glistening with my juices.

Fuck. No way to deny what he was doing to me now.

This was so happening...*revenge fuck here I come!*

Six

Shea

I STARED AT MY FINGER, still warm from Zara's dripping pussy and glistening with her lady jizz. Or whatever the appropriate terminology was. I had a feeling she was wet, but I wasn't expecting Niagara Falls when I slid my finger inside her. When I stroked her G-spot, she gushed, sending her juices dripping down my finger. I was fully convinced if I had a couple minutes to work her over with my entire hand, she'd saturate every inch of her office.

I only said her name—and nothing more, but she melted into my touch when I wrapped my arms around her, pulling her close enough to crush my lips against hers. Her hands laced through my hair as our tongues tangled, dueling for control. I devoured her mouth then moved on to conquer her neck, her chest, and, after ripping her blouse over her head, her breasts. Pausing for just a moment to take in the glorious sight of her full, luscious mounds and creamy ivory skin, I licked my lips before diving in.

She reached behind her back to unhook her bra and unleash her breasts as I began to tease and nibble her nipples into stiff peaks. Her panting breaths fell in my hair as her legs spread and allowed me to press against the heat of her core.

"These jeans have to go," I huffed out between bites, licks, and kisses.

She grunted her agreement, trying to reach down low enough to push them down from where they were already gathered around her knees. No time for that, so I yanked on the cuffs myself, and they fell to the floor in a heap. She fumbled with the buttons on my shirt, preventing me from going back to my feast on her nipples. In the end, she undid two buttons, allowing me to slip the shirt off over my head. Then she went to work on my pants.

It was after-hours at the university, and I was pretty sure this building closed at eight. We started at seven, and I feared nearly an hour had passed already. I had to be at work at nine, so I was pushing my luck. That, and a janitor could always venture in. As if the taboo status of our romp wasn't bad enough, the added threat of being caught made my dick even harder as I rubbed it across the satiny silk of her damp panties.

Her legs wrapped around me, holding me in place like she desperately needed the pressure of my cock against her sex. Back arched, she loosened her grip when I pulled away to slide her panties down. The look in her eyes conveyed a raging inferno of need as I moved down her body. She lost contact with my pelvis, but she was about to meet my tongue, and no woman who met my tongue was ever disappointed.

The gasp that flew out of her mouth when my lips hit her labia could probably be heard in the next building, it was so loud. Surely no one else was still working in the English department this late. There wasn't such thing as an English emergency, right? Their work could wait till tomorrow.

"Shea," she breathed out, trembling as my tongue delved inside her. "Please..."

"Please what?" I groaned as I drank in her juices. Fuck, she tasted divine, a true goddess. I was still wearing my boxer briefs, and my cock felt like it was in a jail made of cotton, so confined, so restricted, so ready to dive into the depths of her wet heat.

"I need—"

"Shh, I'm gonna take care of you," I hummed against her clit.

Her entire body shuddered at that as I circled her clit with the tip of my tongue. Sliding my hands under her hips, I tilted her toward my lips so I could taste more of her, get a deeper angle. This was one feast I wanted to get my fill of, and I couldn't wait to make her explode on my tongue.

Reaching up with one hand, I squeezed a nipple between my thumb and forefinger, causing her to cry out in a mixture of pleasure and pain. My touch only heightened her need, and she ground her hips into my face, coating my nose, my cheeks with her wetness as she built toward her climax.

When she began rocking into me rhythmically, I added a finger, then two, thrusting deep and stroking the G-spot I easily found during my last exploratory mission just minutes ago. *We went from that one wet finger to naked and horizontal on her desk in record time. I wasn't sure an English professor would be impressed by that, but the Physics department surely would be. I was pretty sure we'd already violated a few laws of nature.*

"Come for me, Zara," I growled next to her clit as she began to ride my fingers. I committed the rhythm she preferred to memory. My dick was achingly hard and dripping pre-cum, and I really hoped I would be inside her soon. My boxers were probably as wet as her panties at this point.

"Fuck!" she gasped as she tightened around me. "Oh my god, Shea...." She dragged out the vowel in my name as her orgasm hit her in spasmodic waves, her pussy clenching around me and more fluid gushing into my face. *I practically need a snorkel to keep from drowning in her cum.*

"I wanna fuck you, Zara," I warned, already fumbling for a condom as she came down from her high.

Gasping for air, she managed to beg me for it: "Yes, please, fuck, I need more."

When I looked up at her, her bottom lip was caught in her teeth, her skin flushed from her cheeks down to her breasts. Holy fuck, what a beautiful sight she was, fresh off her climax. I only wanted to see her come again, and this time on my dick.

I rolled the condom down my shaft and moved her to the edge of the desk. Her still trembling legs wrapped around me as I guided the head to her entrance, feeling the wet heat even through the condom. I slid in with very little resistance, the sign of a job well done on my part.

She held on to my sides as I gave her time to adjust to my size, which I'd been told was a little...extra. She didn't seem to mind, though, once she got acclimated, grinding against me just like she had my face.

"You feel incredible," I groaned as I reached maximum

depth. She cried out from the sheer intensity of my cock buried balls-deep inside her. "Can you come again for me?"

"I hope so," she breathed out. "Give me a second."

As soon as the words left her lips, I claimed them again, ravenously chewing and licking and tasting her as I drove deep inside her again and again. I found that rhythm she liked, and soon we were moving as one: a slow, intense tango as the springs inside us coiled tight, ready to explode.

"I've never done this before, never slept with a student," she confessed when I released her lips. "I promise this is my first time."

I bit my lip hard to keep from blowing my load. I needed her to come on my cock. "I don't care if you ever slept with a student or not, just promise me this won't be the last time."

Huh, well, so much for this being a one-night stand and me going back to being a regular student. I had no clue where that came from. I hadn't been compelled to ask a woman to promise me anything for a very long time. Women always seemed to break the promises they made me. Fuck, men did too, for that matter.

"I promise," she rasped out, and the raw sound of her voice shredded me. With one more deep thrust, I lost all control, and she tumbled right after me. We fell over the edge in tandem, riding wave after wave of ecstasy.

And when it was all over, those two words kept echoing in my head on repeat:

I promise.

Zara

Oh my god.

Did I just fuck my high school bully?

His mouth on my pussy felt like heaven, like he had a PhD in cunnilingus. He made me come so easily, I should have been ashamed. No one had ever been able to get me off that fast, not even my ex whom I was married to for ten years. I thought Brandon knew how to push all my buttons, but he was a novice compared to the expert skill of Shea's tongue.

When Shea told me he wanted to fuck me, I practically begged him for his cock. *Shameless little hussy,* my mother would have called me. But my body felt like it would revolt if I waited one more second to let him slide his big, thick dick inside me.

I barely got a look at it, but when he filled me fuller than I've ever felt before, I knew. He not only had the tongue of a god, but the cock of one as well. That G-spot he had found so effortlessly before was an easy target for the length and curvature of his godlike apparatus. My legs wrapped around him, and soon I was meeting each thrust like I might never get fucked like that again.

Because, considering my prior history, there was a damn good chance I wouldn't.

Holy shit, I never knew a revenge fuck could be so sweet! If only he knew I was that fat girl he teased mercilessly when we were in high school.

Only one issue: at the very end, right before we both came, I confessed that I'd never slept with a student before. That was one hundred percent true. I never even considered it, had never been even remotely tempted. Not until Shea.

And then I promised him something...that it wouldn't be the last time we fucked.

Holy shit. Did I really promise him that? What the hell

was I thinking? I couldn't promise him that. We could *never* do this again. In fact, I needed to talk to him about switching sections. We should never even speak again.

Except he's my high school bully. And our twenty-five-year class reunion will be next summer. Fuck, I have to tell him I know him.

After all, what good is a revenge fuck if he doesn't even know he was on the receiving end of it?

Seven

Shea

THERE WAS no way I could avoid being late to class. Judy showed up late to take care of Mom, and then I had to run and refill her prescriptions. Despite being stressed about getting everything done and getting to campus, I was riding a bit of a euphoric wave. I couldn't get Zara Fowler Ames out of my mind.

What happened the other night in her office was possibly the single hottest experience I had ever had. It completely blew my mind. I would have never thought in my teens, twenties, or thirties that the best sex was yet to come, but here I was at forty-two, and this girl I knew from high school was the single best lay I'd ever had.

How could that be?

There was something between us, something that had been missing with each and every other woman I'd ever fucked. I couldn't put my finger on it exactly. The way she responded to my touch, my kiss...it was incredible. Our bodies were so in tune with each other, they were speaking a secret code our brains couldn't possibly translate.

As I strolled into class, wondering if she'd already graded the final draft of my essay with an A, I realized there was still the small matter of our past to contend with. If we were to start dating, and we started talking about where we grew up and went to high school and all that—well, there was no way to deny we were classmates.

And she really didn't seem to know. That was still surprising to me. Maybe she didn't enjoy reliving high school memories, or she had blocked them out. Perhaps she was just hiding it. I was a popular jock in high school, so maybe she thought it was best if she didn't bring it up. Maybe she thought I'd be turned off if I remembered her from high school.

On the contrary, I was pretty damned impressed at how she blossomed. Adulthood looked amazing on her. She was full of confidence, had an advanced degree, and was sexy as hell.

We really needed to keep this just about sex. We really had no business dating in an official capacity anyway—she was my professor, after all. She could get in a lot of trouble if someone found out we'd fucked in her office. That was as good a reason as any to keep our status on the downlow and fuck like bunnies with no strings attached.

Not to mention my situation with my mother, my crazy schedule, my push to finish school and get started on carving out a new life for myself. I didn't need any more distractions. Hot sex wasn't a distraction, though. It was a stress reliever, and fuck yes did I need more of that in my life!

When I pushed the classroom door open, quite pleased

with the solution I'd come up with, I could hear Zara's voice booming out toward the rows of students. Class was well underway, and I was interrupting. Surely she wouldn't mind. I could just stroll on over to the last row of desks and pretend like everything was just fine.

"Mr. Hunt," she snapped, her stare landing squarely on me along with her voice.

I stopped dead in my tracks about halfway to the back row. When I turned to meet her gaze, I stiffened. She did not look pleased.

"I don't accept latecomers in my classroom," she said in a neutral, monotone voice. "Furthermore, this policy is clearly stated in my syllabus, which you would have known if you'd bothered to read it. So, I need you to leave my classroom at this time; however, you may return and speak with me after class if you'd like. I do have your paper to return."

Her eyes looked weaponized, like they might stab right through me if I didn't get my ass out of her classroom right this moment. I shrugged, not missing the snickers of a few of my fellow students, who were obviously delighted to see the old dude in their class get reamed out by the teacher. Then I pivoted on my heel and casually strolled right back out.

I thought about leaving campus. I'd busted my ass to get there today—and I wasn't trying to disrespect Zara at all. Just, you know, being the old dude in the class meant I had a lot of life shit to deal with. I wasn't some twenty-something full-time college student who literally had two responsibilities in life beyond basic self-care: showing up for fucking class and doing the fucking work.

But I wanted my paper back.

And I wanted to talk to her.

Hopefully smooth things over.

There was something hot as hell about Zara Fowler Ames when she was angry, though, and just the mere thought of those stabby dark eyes was enough to bring my cock to life. *Down boy*, I issued the command as I headed downstairs to the little vestibule at the bottom with vending machines. I'd grab a snack and wait class out. It was only an hour. I was sure I could find something to entertain myself.

As soon as class was over, I sauntered right back down the hall, watching my fellow students file out the classroom door.

"Dude, you got pwned," some lanky kid with a silly grin said as he passed. His buddy burst into laughter, and the sound of their chuckles carried down the hall.

When the classroom was empty, I slipped back inside to find Zara closing down the computer and gathering up her things. "Ah, Mr. Hunt. You decided to return."

"I'm sorry I was late," I apologized, and I was sincere. I had a bit of reputation for being a clown in high school—but she didn't remember that side of me, right? "I needed to run a few errands before class, and time just slipped away."

"You don't need to apologize to me," she fired back. "It's your grade that will suffer if you miss the material. But I did grade your final draft, and I didn't see a vast improvement over your first draft, I'm sorry to say."

She flipped over a stapled essay with a huge, glaring F neatly written and circled at the top. The margins had fewer comments than before, but her red pen had still gotten a workout.

"I really hope you're not wasting your time and money in this course," she said, her lips pursed. "I'm getting paid either way, of course. But if you're not willing to put forth any effort, then—"

"I tried!" Frustrated, I slumped in one of the desks in the first row and sighed, scrubbing my hands down my face. Then I tried flashing her that charming grin that won her over before, but it was clear that tactic would not work this go-around. "I came to you for help—*twice*—and apparently you weren't able to help me."

"Didn't I, though? Help you, I mean?" Her gaze narrowed as it landed on me, and if I wasn't mistaken, the edges of her lips curled up ever so slightly.

I glanced around to make sure no one was within earshot. The footsteps and murmurs of people in the hallway as they made their way to classes filled my ears, but they weren't paying attention to us. As I took a step closer to her, the combination of her scent and heat practically walloped me over the head. *Holy hell, why does she have to smell so damn good?* Looking at her and smelling her essence made me feel like I was standing, ravenous and my mouth watering, in front of a decadent buffet but not allowed to have a single bite.

"Are you trying to say that our time together the other night wasn't worthy of a little...bump in my grade?" I licked my lip for emphasis in case she needed a little visual reminder of what I was referring to.

A scowl tightened her features—yet, despite that, she still looked radiant. "Are you trying to use what happened between us to influence your grade? Look, Shea Hunt," she practically spat in my face, "I know who you are. I haven't forgotten the vile things you said to me when we were in school. I will be grading your papers in a purely professional manner—and failing work shall receive a failing grade. Do I make myself clear?"

I struggled to keep my jaw from dropping. "You knew who I was the other night too, didn't you? What, you wanted to see what you were missing out on in high school?"

"You better forget the other night ever happened, Mr. Hunt," she seethed. "Not only will it *never* happen again, but passing this class won't happen either if you don't keep it to yourself. Now, get out of my classroom before I call campus security and have you forcibly removed."

Zara

I watched him go, my heart racing and my palms sweating, no matter how cool, calm and collected I appeared to be as I handed Mr. Hunt his marching orders. When he disappeared into the hallway, barely registering any reaction at all to my scolding—without a shred of disappointment and only a hint of surprise—I let out the breath I'd been holding.

A lot had happened in the past forty-eight hours, but the biggest thing was that the morning following my after-hours rendezvous with Shea, my department chair, Alan, was lurking outside my office when I arrived. The scene replayed in my head, sending a shiver through my entire body.

"What do you want?" I didn't even look at him, just focused on unlocking my office door.

"I understand you had a meeting with a student in your intensive writing seminar last night, Zara," he sneered,

following me into my office as I flipped off the light and went to fire up my computer.

"How would you know that? Do you have cameras installed or something?" I still didn't bother to look at him as I set down my things, settled into my desk chair and began to get my files in order for the day.

"No, but that's a good idea." A sardonic laugh drifted into the space between us, sending a chill down my spine. Alan made my skin positively crawl, but when I closed my eyes, I could nearly smell the heavy scent of sex still lingering in the air around my desk.

Holy fuck. Am I imagining that?

"If you must know, the facilities coordinator was on the floor last night around the time your, ahem, student left, and he reported said student was zipping up his pants as he walked away from your office."

The blood in my veins froze, but I wasn't about to let Alan see his statement had that effect on me, so I scoffed. "What is that supposed to mean? Maybe he'd just used the restroom."

"He described the student—forties, tall, well-built, salt and pepper hair, so I took the liberty of looking him up in this semester's student list. There are only four students in their forties taking English classes on campus this semester, and the only male is Shea Hunt. He's in your intensive writing class."

I rolled my eyes. What was this asshole's problem? Who goes to this much effort to get their colleague in trouble?

"Will you please cut to the chase, Alan? Are you accusing me of something?"

"Should I be?" he fired back. "Was Shea Hunt in your office last night?"

I saw no reason to deny it. Faculty often met with students after hours, though it typically wasn't one-on-one at night in their offices. Not unheard of, though. And we are both adults, for fuck's sake. It's not like he's some eighteen-year-old kid.

"I advised Mr. Hunt with regard to an essay he's writing for my class," I calmly explained. "And that's it. I have no idea what was going on with his zipper—perhaps he realized it was down when he left my office. I really have no interest in such matters."

Liar! *a voice inside my head called out.*

"I'll be keeping an eye on Mr. Hunt myself," Alan warned. "Oh, and just so you know, the committee is meeting next Friday about your dossier. I'm sure you wouldn't want me to withdraw my stamp of approval—I am the committee chair, after all. I'm sure if I found reason to question your integrity and professionalism, the other committee members would be interested in learning why."

"Are you threatening me, Alan?"

"It's not a threat," his voice oozed with slimy condescension, "it's a promise."

Fuck. That. Asshole.

After he left my office, I made a vow that I would come clean to Shea about knowing who he was, grade his rewrite fairly, and put on a chastity belt if it meant keeping myself from fucking him again.

Shea

Holy hell. What just happened in there?

I thought I'd found my in for a passing grade and a little diversion to keep me entertained and my balls empty for the rest of the semester, but Zara just confessed to remembering me from high school. I was a jerk to her. The full details of what I said or did to her were sketchy, but I had a feeling it was bad.

For shits and giggles, on my way home, I called up Tony Manelli, who was my best bud back in high school. He was the shooting guard to my power forward on the basketball team. We both shared various records for numbers of points and assists. We were also crowned co-prom kings our senior year. Apparently there was a tie in the voting, so they decided to let us share the honor. Considering everything we shared on and off the court, it made perfect sense. I would have never made it through our senior year without him after what happened in my family.

He had also stuck around our small hometown a half-hour outside the city where the university was. We got together every once in a while, but he was on his second marriage, and he'd had a whole new set of kids with his new wife. That meant he was busy being Sports Dad at baseball and soccer games almost every night and weekend.

"Hey, if it isn't Three-Point Shea!" Tony's raspy voice greeted me.

"Ton' the Clone," I dragged out his high school nickname as well. This was our usual routine. He was called The Clone because he was so fast on the court, and so good at defense, it was like there must be two of him.

"Well, what's up, buddy? I know you didn't call me for nothin'." His boisterous laugh gurgled down the line.

"Well, you know I always want to catch up with my bro, but I do have something kind of weird to ask you." *No point in beating around the bush, am I right?*

"What's that?"

"Is this a good time to talk?"

"Kids are in bed, and the wife is watching some dumb-ass show...*Bridgerton* or some shit?"

"Oh, I heard about that. You're probably gonna get laid later," I teased him.

"You think? Oh, I'm down with that. For sure." He laughed again.

I cleared my throat, trying to decide how to approach this. "Hey, I think I told you I'm back in school this semester, working on my business degree."

"Oh, that's right, man! How's that goin'?"

"Pretty well, pretty well," I answered. "But you're never gonna believe who my English professor is..."

"Someone we went to school with?" he guessed.

"Yeah, not sure if you remember her...Zara Fowler?" I threw the name out at him, seeing how he would react.

"Zara Fowler, Zara Fowler...Zara Cowler?" he shot back.

Cowler?

Oh. Like Cow. Got it.

"I forgot we called her that." I couldn't keep the disappointment out of my voice.

"So, what's she like now? Fatter?" He laughed again. "Hillary Mason got fat too, and she was the hottest cheerleader on the squad. She almost sucked my dick on the bus ride back from Columbus our senior year, you know."

"I know, you've told me at least a hundred times." I rolled my eyes. I was pretty sure "almost sucked my dick" was more like she fell asleep in his lap, and her mouth drooled a bit on his crotch.

"So, Zara Fowler is your English professor?" Tony brought me back around to the original topic.

"Yeah, man. Isn't that weird? She looks great, by the way. She's still a curvy girl, but she wears it well."

Laughter spilled out of Tony's mouth and down the line, almost contagious. "Wow, Hunt, you sound like you wanna fuck her. That would be pretty hilarious after what we did to her in high school."

Now we were getting somewhere. That was the type of intel I was hoping Tony would give.

"What did we do to her in high school?"

He scoffed. "What? You don't remember?" His voice lowered. "Well, you did have a lot going on our senior year..."

"Right. So I only remember bits and pieces." Did I block out some of this stuff due to the accident? I knew I was a jerk to her a few times but couldn't recall any specific interactions. "Hey, man, can you jog my memory?"

Eight

Zara

ANOTHER NIGHT AT HOME, alone, grading papers and eating leftovers for dinner. *Livin' that divorcée life. Sigh.* I was on my third paper of the night when my phone buzzed. I looked down to see a notification from the app I used to communicate with my students so they didn't have my actual phone number.

User3784: *It's Shea. Listen, we need to talk.*

Electricity bolted down my spine as soon as I spotted those letters: S-H-E-A. My heart raced as a sudden ache in my core reminded me what it felt like to be filled with his cock.

No! I chided myself. *That cock is strictly off-limits.* It didn't matter how damn good it felt. It didn't matter if it was the best sex of my life—*spoiler alert: it was*—I was not going to risk my job to fuck that asshole again. And I did mean *asshole*. Exhibit A being our entire four years of high school.

But I did need to text him back because it was the professorial thing to do.

Dr.Ames: *Is this about class?*

User3784: *Not exactly.*

Fuck. I should tell him I am only willing to talk to him if it relates to class. It wouldn't surprise me at all if Alan could hack into this messaging system, so I wasn't about to say anything that would get me in trouble.

I could call him, I realized. I had his number. Students only had professors' cell numbers if they chose to give them out—yeah, I wasn't about to let those students harass me on my cell phone all hours of the day and night. But the class roster had a contact number for every student. I could try Shea's. Alan couldn't hack into that. *At least he better not be able to!*

I looked up Shea's number in my course management system, and before I could stop myself, I was dialing his number. He answered on the second ring.

"Zara?"

"Listen, we can't talk on the app."

"Why not?"

A sigh puffed out of my mouth. "Because the janitor saw you leaving my office the other night, and you were zipping up your fly."

"Oh, damn!" he gasped and then chuckled. "Sorry about that."

"It's not funny," I scolded him. "The janitor went and tattled to my chair, who is the head of my tenure committee, and they are voting on my tenure on Friday. He threatened me—"

"Wait, what?"

"He said if he found out anything was going on between me and a student, he wasn't going to approve my tenure. He even figured out who you were, so I know he's watching us."

"So that's why you were such a bitch to me in class today!" There was no mistaking the victory in his voice. "I mean besides figuring out who I am..."

"I was strictly professional and treated you as I would any student," I defended myself. "Your paper sucked, Shea. I wasn't lying about that."

"I want to talk to you..."

"We're talking now."

"I mean in person. I... Zara, I owe you a huge apology."

My spine prickled. *What did he just say?*

"I'm listening," was all I said.

"Can I see you? I promise I won't take up too much of your time."

I sighed. *No* was right on the tip of my tongue, but— that D was pretty fucking spectacular. If he apologized for his behavior in high school, did that mean I got another shot at it? I mean *of* it?

"I don't know if it's a good idea for you to come here." Maybe I could weasel out of it. Did I really want Shea Hunt to know where I lived, anyway?

"I can't invite you here," he said flatly.

"Oh, is that so? Are you married, Shea? I mean, I probably should have asked you that before, but—"

"I'm not married."

"Things got out of hand before I got a chance..." What was I doing? Was I actually considering this? Yes, the D was a powerful entity, a thing of beauty and pleasure that I'd been sorely lacking in the past few years since my divorce, but surely I could be a fucking grown-up and resist the siren call of that thing.

Who am I kidding? It wasn't just the D that was driving my racing heart and throbbing clit. Shea was a masterpiece. From that chiseled, scruff-lined jaw, to his intense aquamarine eyes, to that firm, round butt and those muscular arms and legs. Fuck me sideways, he was a gorgeous specimen.

But if he was married, I didn't want him.

"I am not fucking around with you if you're married."

"Hey, I told you, I'm not married. I promise. Look on my student record—it tells you my marital status on there, doesn't it? I just can't host at my house, that's all."

"Why, you have kids at home?"

"I have a daughter who is grown up and out of the house, but, no, that's not why—"

"Then why is it?" I persisted. I didn't like how evasive he was being.

"Let me come over, and I'll explain..."

"I can't do this, Shea. If you want to apologize, just do it right here on the phone. We're both adults."

"Please, just give me your address. I don't even have to come inside. We can talk in the driveway if you want. *You're* not married, are you? Kids at home?"

"Divorced. No kids," I fired back.

"Please?"

Shea

What would my seventeen-year-old self think if I told him at age forty-two I'd be calling up Zara Cowler—god, I'd forgotten we called her that—and begging her to see me?

"I'll be on my best behavior, I promise." That was my last-ditch effort. I wasn't going to *actually* beg.

"I can't, Shea. I'm sorry."

And with that, she hung up.

Damn it. I was sure between what she remembered about me from high school and what her stupid boss was pulling, there was no way I was going to get a second chance with her. I still couldn't believe how mind-blowing the sex was. If I'd known she was such a vixen, I would have taken my chances being ridiculed by my friends and bedded her in high school...

Fuck, that was mean. I shouldn't say or think shit like that. I hurt her feelings. I was cruel, and it was completely unacceptable. *I shouldn't even consider trying to change her mind. I don't deserve a second chance with her.*

Three seconds later, my phone buzzed:

614 Crimson Court. Text me when you get here.

* * *

Crimson Court—wasn't familiar with that street, but when I put it in my GPS, I saw it was part of a swanky housing development in an affluent neighborhood. Guess that professor salary wasn't treating her too badly—or perhaps she made out in her divorce. When I pulled up and took in her two-story modern home with its huge windows and welcoming porch, I shrugged. It was a lot nicer than my little two-bedroom bungalow I shared with my mother. I wasn't going to feel too sorry for her.

But I *was* going to deliver a kick-ass apology because I was a gentleman—or I'd learned to be one since high school anyway. And she *did* deserve it.

I texted her from my truck, as promised, a simple *Here.*

Coming out, she texted back.

She appeared, seconds later, in the garage as the door slowly rose to reveal her in all her stunning glory—*wait a sec, are those sweatpants?*

Oh, I'm definitely not getting laid tonight.

She was wearing baggy sweatpants with wide legs, fuzzy slippers, a loose-fitting hoodie partially unzipped (not sure if she had a bra on, to be honest), and her hair was not the sleek style I typically saw in the classroom. Instead, it was pulled back with some sort of fabric headband. Completing the look was a pair of glasses.

"Hey." She gestured to herself. "You're the one who insisted on seeing me. Well, here I am."

I had to laugh at her openness. It was appealing, really, to see a woman who didn't feel like she needed to paint herself up or squeeze into form-fitting clothes for a man. On the other hand, maybe her lack of effort signified she was resigned to not getting laid tonight.

"Can we go inside?" I asked. "Surely you don't want the neighbors being nosy..."

"Anything you have to say to me, you can say right here," she said through clenched teeth, like she was really struggling to stand her ground.

I shrugged. I was lucky she even agreed to see me. *Beggars can't be choosers and all that.*

"Fine. Zara, I...I did remember who you were after the first class we had. But I had forgotten how horribly my friends and I treated you, until my buddy—Tony Manelli, if you remember him—pointed it out—"

"You told Tony Manelli we fucked?"

I scoffed, "No! Of course not. I told him I was in your English class..."

"Oh."

"And he reminded me of the cruel nickname we gave you and some other stuff, like what happened with the homecoming dance, and, Zara...I..." I shook my head, realizing this was hopeless. There was no way she would forgive me, and there was no fucking way I was going to pass her class.

"Why are you here?" Her hands fisted at her hips as she stared me down.

"I felt bad about how we treated you...how *I* treated you," I admitted, stepping closer to her. She stood firm, feet slightly spread, hip cocked, lips thinned.

I didn't care that she was wearing sweats—they couldn't hide her mouthwatering curves from me. And her glasses only made her look more intellectual and sexy as fuck. I was hard as a rock remembering what it felt like to be inside her, and I wanted nothing more than to relive that moment when my cock first slid into her tight pussy.

I stepped close enough that I could smell her, that exotic floral scent filling my nostrils and making my heart pump blood straight to my cock. It was standing at attention, straining against the zipper in my pants. "Zara," I breathed in, close enough to nuzzle her neck. "I'm sorry. Can you ever forgive me?"

Her breath hitched as her body tensed, and her lips went from being clenched tight to her bottom lip being caught between her teeth. "Shea..." was all she could get out as my hot breath on her neck sent goosebumps racing up her arms. I could just see the effects of my proximity on her forearms, where her sweatshirt cuffs were pushed up a few inches above her wrists.

"I can't do this," she breathed out as I stroked my hand down her cheek and lifted her chin, turning her to face me.

"You already have," I reminded her, "and promised me it wouldn't be the last time..."

"You can't hold me to something I promised when I was on the verge of orgasm!"

"I can't?" A breathy laugh fell from my lips and landed in the hollow of her collarbones as I bent to trail kisses up her neck to just behind her ear. Her body gave way to me, her knees wobbling as she fell under my spell.

"Shea...I'm your professor. I can't—"

"You want me just as bad as I want you," I posited. "I could write an entire essay on how your body is begging mine to take you right now."

Her eyes flashed open at that, glimmering like stars. "Is that so?"

"I may not be a poet like you are, but I know poetry when I see it, hear it. That catch in your voice is a tiny plea. That pinkness on your skin is a blushing rosebud, preparing to unfurl." I swallowed down a breath as my eyes trailed over her body and my fingers loosened the zipper of her hoodie. There was no bra underneath, just large, squeez-able, lickable mounds of perfection. "And those nipples are hard as diamonds, Zara. Please don't try to deny what I'm doing to you."

"Fuck...you really have no respect for authority, do you?" she gasped as I threaded my fingers through her hair and pulled her mouth to mine, where I devoured her lips, tenderly at first and then with more aggression. I felt her need to be claimed, to be taken, to be held, and I wanted to give her that with every fiber of my being.

"Just let me take you inside and fuck you, Zara. I promise you will feel one hundred and twenty percent better after you've come..."

Nine

Zara

I DIDN'T KNOW how I let him talk me into this. How did we start off with me in my sweatpants, standing my ground, and then moments later, I'm leading him inside like I placed an order for the D, and he's here to deliver it? Like it was all my idea, when it was his, his, and more his!

Did he really apologize to me for his behavior when we were growing up? Did he just seduce me while I was wearing literally the least sexy outfit in my closet? On a scale of zero sexiness to ten sexiness, these sweatpants are like negative five. This was turning out to be such a bizarre night.

Once the door swung open, he was all hands, fingers, lips and tongue; the urgency that took over his body was almost alarming. But something about it reached deep inside me, triggering what might have been a latent fantasy I'd never been able to admit having.

Had I been craving this all along? Having a student ravish me?

No, I would never be interested in the twenty-somethings who filled my classroom semester after semester. I was old enough to have given birth to them. That did not appeal to me.

But perhaps the idea of someone my age, sitting in my classroom...eyes raking over me as I lectured, jotting down notes, perhaps fantasizing about what it might be like to bed the professor...

There was definitely something titillating about that.

"Zara," he growled once we made it to my bedroom. "I want to see you. I want to see all of you."

That shy, nervous, ashamed-of-my-body girl I'd been twenty-five years ago when he ridiculed me was gone forever. Now I stood tall, proud, confident in my curves. He hadn't seen me naked yet—we were still mostly clothed when we fucked in my office. I might have been wearing sweatpants, but underneath was a voluptuous goddess. And he was going to lose his mind when he saw what I had to offer him.

Two words ground out as he slowly unzipped my hoodie and slid it off my arms, leaving my heaving breasts ready for his lips, tongue, and teeth: "Fuck me..." He couldn't move any further until he'd addressed my nipples. He said it himself: they were begging for his mouth.

While he was sucking and licking my breasts, my hands snaked down his strong abs to the fly on his pants. I was dying to get a look at this monster between his legs. I had already felt it inside me—I had a pretty good idea what it would look like, but there was just something about actually seeing it.

It took some finessing to unbutton his pants and pull

down the zipper because the caged beast was so insistent to get out. And when it sprang out at me in all its glory, I fell to my knees in front of him, eager to wrap my lips around him.

He looked down at me with such hunger in his eyes, it took my breath away. "You're sure about this?"

I wasn't. At least my brain wasn't. Of course, the rest of my body was rarin' to go. I hadn't wanted a man this badly, well, ever, if I was being honest with myself. What was it about this guy that revved my engine? I wasn't able to control myself around him. If the sweatpants didn't deter either of us, what hope did I ever have of resisting?

I slowly nodded, my gaze locked on his as my tongue darted out and just barely, almost imperceptibly flicked at the tip of his cock. His whole body seized at that barest touch, his thighs going rigid beneath my grip on either side of him.

My hands moved up to his ass, squeezing his firm muscles in my hands, kneading a groan right out of his mouth. Or maybe it was because I chose that moment to engulf his head in my warm mouth and trace the ridge underneath with my tongue. A desperate breath slipped out next as I raked my lips, soaked with saliva, down his shaft all the way to his balls before cupping them in my right hand as I continued to squeeze his ass cheek in my left.

"Fuck, you're killing me, Zara..."

It was only a small fraction of what he deserved after being so cruel to me in high school. I should have brought him to the very edge of climax, as close as you can get to the point of no return without falling over, and then sent him away, banished him from my house, and punished him with a failing grade in my class. But I just kept thinking about how sinfully delicious his cock tasted in my mouth and how it filled me so completely, so exquisitely the other night.

Why should I suffer just to make him suffer?

We could both get what we wanted out of this situation.

And, in the end, if I still wanted retribution, well, there was always the matter of his grade.

I took him deep in my throat then, choking myself on his massive length, spit nearly spraying out of my mouth as I pressed my lips firmly into him and stroked up to his tip before plunging down again. He reached down and ripped the headband out of my hair, sending my silky dark tresses spilling into my face.

"You want my cum down your throat or in your pussy?" he growled after I bobbed up and down on him a few more times, his balls tightening with each pass.

Well, I wanted both, to be honest, but I supposed that wasn't one of the choices?

Pity.

I didn't know if he was the type of guy who could get it up over and over again at our age—my ex-husband was older and could barely rise to the occasion once, let alone multiple times in one night. But I was going to take my chances because I wanted to taste him. I wanted to hold this power over him, the power to make him come with my hands and mouth. I'd already done it with my pussy...

"I warned you," he ground out as I slurped his cock with stronger suction, my hands stroking up and down following behind my mouth.

A few more pumps and I knew I had him. It had been ages since I'd brought a man to climax this way, and I was feeling like a goddamn goddess, nearly drunk on power. My cheeks hollowed out as I sucked him with all I had, his control disintegrating with each and every stroke.

"Yes, oh fucking fuck," plus some unintelligible groans fired out of Shea's mouth as I prepared myself to swallow his cum. Just when I thought my jaw might crack, his cock throbbed and spasmed, shooting thick spurts of salty, creamy goodness down my throat. His hips jerked as he drained his balls, my lungs heaving as I struggled to take it all before gasping for breath.

He stilled, his cock rock-hard in my mouth, his grip on my chin loosening as he came down from his high. As soon as he regained his composure, he scooped me up—this heavy, curvy body—and threw me down on the bed. "I have to taste you," was his excuse for manhandling me as he forced my thighs apart and climbed between them.

"Fuck, Shea, give me a—"

"Shut up," he commanded before his lips attacked mine, chewing and licking and sucking every molecule of residual cum from my mouth. "Tasting me on your lips is... fuck...I need to lick you down here now..."

He slid down my body like a man possessed, but when he reached my crown of dark, coiled hair, he sucked in an audible breath. "Your scent...holy fuck, you smell like pure, unadulterated desire..." To confirm, he swiped his finger up my slit like he did in my office just a few days before. "Zara...did sucking my cock really make you this wet?"

I whimpered as he shoved the finger into his mouth and licked it clean. "You could bottle this up and sell it, Zara. It's the very essence of arousal. Absolutely fucking primal." He buried his nose between my lips and ran his tongue up the seam, stopping right before my clit.

I winced. I needed him now. Was he going to get me back for my tease? *Turnabout is fair play and all that?*

"I love the way you're squirming for me..." His voice was low, raspy, rumbling right through my core like faraway thunder. "You were such a good girl to let me come in your mouth. But you were always a good girl, weren't you, Zara? A straight-A student—weren't you valedictorian?"

I nodded, my voice barely a squeak as he circled my clit with the tip of his tongue. "Mmhmm."

Every single nerve in my body was on high alert, perched on the edge of a lush valley, longing for the exquisite release where it crested the horizon. "Shea, please —please don't make me wait."

"I wasn't a good boy in school. You remember that, right?"

Another squeaky nod.

"I liked to push teachers' buttons. Hey, do you remember that time Mr. Singleton sent me to the principal's office for stapling his gradebook together? That was fuckin' hilarious—"

"Shea..." I did not want to relive high school right now. He was going to kill my lady wood if he did that.

"I still like to push teachers' buttons. Mmm...like this one..." He sucked my clit into his mouth, savoring it like a truffle before releasing it, leaving me quaking on the bed. "Do you want to come, Dr. Ames?" He dragged a finger up my slit, barely flicking my clit.

A deep ache was beginning to grow in my core as my thighs trembled and my heart rate soared. "Don't be cruel to me...I thought you came here to apologize."

"You're right..." He lifted up to his knees, surveying my body with his lusty, steely stare. "Seeing you helpless and wound up this tight has made me hard again already." He reached down and fisted his cock, which was as described. "Do you want to come on my tongue or on my cock?"

Remembering the exquisite pleasure of him stroking inside me made my decision easy. My thighs fell open, ready to receive him as my hand rose to touch my own clit, trying to relieve a little of the pent-up pressure.

"No." He gripped my hand. "You'll wait until I say you can come."

"I thought I was in charge here," I whimpered, but it certainly didn't sound very authoritative. How could I be enjoying this? This loss of control? My entire body was so weak, waiting for him to tear me apart and put me back together again.

"Like I said, I've always had authority issues. You know," he teased the head of his cock against my clit, making me bite my bottom lip to stifle a moan, "I thought maybe I was so drawn to you because you're my professor. I mean, it is pretty hot, even if it's cliché, right?"

I nodded as he glided the tip up through my folds, collecting my wetness on his satiny skin.

"But that's not actually the whole truth, Zara," he confessed.

"It's not?"

"The whole truth," he ripped open the condom package with his teeth and poised it over his glistening crown, "the whole truth is that I wanted you even back then."

"Back then?"

"In high school..."

"But—"

"I always appreciated a curvy figure," he admitted. "I just didn't want my friends to make fun of me, so I was extra cruel to you. It was wrong. I was a jerk, and I don't deserve the time of day from you now—"

My body seized, warring against itself. Did my anger destroy my desire, or did it just ramp it up a notch?

"You're even more beautiful now," he continued as he rolled the condom down his cock, "and I wanna make you come over and over again. I don't think I would ever get tired of seeing you riding waves of ecstasy, Zara. Let me make it up to you—the way I treated you—"

"Okay," I murmured, my voice swallowed up by a combination of need and emotion. What was this man doing to me? I never expected to see this side of him. I thought this was about sex...about scratching each other's itches. I never expected him to care about what happened in the past. Or even admit to it.

"I'm going to fuck you now, Zara, however you want it. However you need it. Whatever will make that pretty pussy explode on my cock. You tell me what you need..."

I sucked in a breath and nodded as his thick, throbbing cock began to slide into me, inch by inch, stealing the breath I'd just taken. "Shea..."

"That's it; take it all, every inch... Let me know when you're ready for me to move."

He stilled inside me, allowing me to fill my lungs and wrap my arms around his waist. My fingers stroked down the muscles of his back, sighing as that familiar need urged my hips to move against him. "I'm ready..."

He stroked slowly, deeply, grinding into me at a steady pace as he gauged my reaction, attuned to every breath, every sigh, each time my eyes rolled back into my head in pleasure. He could read me, my body, without me saying a word, and by the time I could voice my desire, he was already doing it. Faster? He had already sped up the tempo. Deeper? He was angling our bodies so he could reach the deepest depths. I was about to ask him to kiss me when he claimed my lips, his tongue eager to dance with mine.

"Let go," he groaned in my ear as he broke my kiss. "Let go, Zara, give me that climax. Come on my cock…"

And just like that…I did…

Ten

Shea

I DID NOT INTEND to spend the night. *Shit*. At least I remembered to call out sick after our second round of fucking. My boss wasn't too pleased with me, but she'd get over it.

The clock said five forty-three when I finally got my eyes to focus on it. I had plenty of time to run home and check on Mom, shower, and get back to campus for my first class. I hardly got any sleep on Tuesdays—what I got last night in Zara's bed was more than usual because I was supposed to be working until five o'clock.

Looks like I wore her the fuck out, I observed as I slid my legs off the mattress till my feet hit the floor. I apparently scared the cat because he bolted from his spot at the end of the bed and raced down the hall. After a stop in the bathroom, I dug through the pile of clothes on the floor—including those infamous sweatpants Zara was wearing last night—until I retrieved my jeans. After pulling them up my legs and zipping them, I yanked on my shirt and bent to press a kiss to Sleeping Beauty's cheek.

She didn't stir, not even when I lingered there, sucking in her delicious scent like I may never smell it again. I hustled out the door as dawn began to crack the sky open. My car's windshield was a little frosted over. *How is it cold enough to frost already?*

Checking my messages, I waited for the car to heat up, the windows to defrost, and my brain to wake up. Images from the previous night bounced around my mind like pin balls, lighting up various areas of my body as I realized Zara was imprinted on me: her touch, her smell, her essence.

What the hell was I going to do about her? I hoped she didn't think I was doing all this just to pass her class. I really enjoyed myself last night—but I understood we had to play it cool on campus so her stupid boss would approve her tenure. I didn't really understand how it all worked, but I knew it was important for her career, and I didn't want to fuck up her career any more than I wanted her to fuck up mine.

I guess we both have plenty of skin in the game, then?

As I backed out of her driveway, my eyes caught on a dark sedan parked on the curb a few houses up. As soon as I began to pull away, I watched out my rearview mirror as the sedan came to life, its headlights shining into my eyes. A single male occupant tossed back what looked like the rest of his coffee before inching his way down the street after me.

What the hell is this motherfucker doing? Following me?

That'd be a big hell no from me. I sped up, whipping around a curve and narrowly missing a garbage truck out on an early morning run. The blare of its horn probably woke up every sleeping person in a six-block radius, including Zara. I kept going, dodging a man who was out walking his dog in the early morning light, and then taking another side street. I had no idea where I was—all these classy neighborhoods looked the same with their curving streets and perfectly manicured lawns.

My heart pounded when I saw the dark sedan was still behind me. I held my breath and floored the gas pedal, going right through the next four-way stop and jerking the wheel hard to turn left at the second stop. I went around a curve, then took another side street heading toward the interstate. When I looked up into the mirror, it seemed I'd lost my tail.

Motherfucker!

* * *

"Mama?" I called out when I twisted the key in the lock. "Mama, you awake?"

"She's still asleep," Judy said, coming around the corner to greet me. She was wearing a thick cardigan with a turtleneck underneath and those stretchy pants older ladies wear. She'd been awake for a while. "I gave her her meds at five since you didn't come home."

"I'm sorry about that," I apologized and whipped out my wallet. "Here, let me pay you for staying over—"

She waved her hand, brushing off my attempt to rectify the situation. "It's fine, Shea. But listen, I have a procedure coming up tomorrow. I'm going to need a few days off while I recover. Sorry for the short notice; I didn't know until yesterday when I saw the doctor."

"Oh." I hoped she was okay. She looked positively petrified to tell me she wouldn't be able to care for my mother while she convalesced. She was an elderly woman too—she had her own health issues to deal with. I was lucky she'd always been so healthy, to be honest. "Is there anything I can do to help?"

"No, sweet boy. Please make other arrangements for the rest of the week. My daughter is coming from Houston to help me." That last part made her smile.

"No worries," I assured her. "I'll figure something out."

Fuck, my boss was going to kill me if I missed any more work. And how was I going to be on campus all day if Judy couldn't stop by to feed Mom lunch?

"I'll see you tonight," she said as she gathered up her purse and the Bible she always carried with her. "You'll be here this time?"

"I'm sorry again about last night. I stepped out to take care of some stuff around eight, thought I'd be back before work, but—"

"See you tonight," she repeated, smiled, and she was out the door before I could say another word.

I stepped down the hallway toward my mother's room, and sure enough, her small frame formed a lump under the quilt she kept on her bed that had been passed down through the generations. I believe her grandmother made it, but it might have been her great-grandmother. That thing had certainly stood the test of time—a lot better than my mother's brain.

She started slipping after we lost Caroline. It was just a little bit at first. She would spend days in her room, though, imprisoned by a deep, dark depression. The only person she wanted was my dad.

And then we lost him too.

Zara

The sunlight hit my face when I rolled toward the window. That meant no one was blocking it. Shea was gone. My fingertips trailed across the sheets, cool to my touch. He left a while ago. With a heavy sigh, I pulled myself out of bed.

Why the fuck do I keep fucking him?

I couldn't believe I was willing to put my entire career in jeopardy to fuck my high school bully. It was ridiculous. Infuriating. I really needed to stay away from this guy, but with him being in my class—

Oh, maybe I could get him to switch classes. That would solve everything, right? We were only a few weeks into the semester.

Today was my late day. I didn't have any morning classes, so I typically slept in and did some grading and mainlining coffee before dragging myself to campus. I set myself up in the recliner in my living room, feet propped up, the infamous gray sweats bunched up around my calves as I positioned my computer in my lap and began to download my students' assignments from the course management system.

Their second assignment was to write an informative piece about a current topic that interested them. I was anxious to see if their citation style and mechanics had improved since our first essay. The first one I pulled up was Shea's—pure coincidence, but as soon as I saw his name at the top of the MLA-style document, my heart seized up for a beat and then galloped like it was racing toward some phantom finish line that didn't actually exist.

How could just the mere sight of his name affect me this way? It was completely beyond my control.

I tried to screw my head on straight, get into English professor mode. I didn't deserve tenure if I couldn't put my out-of-control libido aside and be an impartial grader.

His essay was about Alzheimer's disease. It seemed like a random topic for someone our age to be interested in, but his three-page essay was well thought out. He presented some logical arguments for allowing expanded drug studies using a risk-benefit analysis for patients who are otherwise going to pass—and what was their quality of life in the meantime? One particular passage stood out to me:

To be a living, breathing person who doesn't recognize their own loved ones—that is not a life. That is a prison sentence.

Even though his paper was informative and serious, that tiny expression of passion surprised me. His writing had improved over the first essay, and I typed some notes using the comment feature. I'd be grading these electronically, unlike the first assignment.

After I made it through four papers, it was time to head to campus. I got myself ready, wearing a plaid skirt, tights, knee-high boots and a thick cardigan since the weather decided to finally let autumn do her thing. Still riding a high from all those orgasms Shea gave me the night before, I drove to campus and parked in a faculty spot near my office building.

I greeted a few colleagues as I made my way to the Ivory Tower, then I unlocked my office door. I only had time to grab a few things before I was due across campus at my one o'clock class. A folded piece of paper with the corner tucked under my keyboard caught my eye. My blood ran cold when I saw the words written in red ink:

I know what you did last night. See me in my office ASAP. Alan.

Fuck.

Double fuck.

I rushed out of the office, down the hallway to the stairwell and flew down multiple flights of stairs until I was back outdoors in the late September sunshine. It suddenly felt like the sun was bearing down on me, summer returning with a vengeance as my heart raced and I tried to figure out what to do.

Walking so fast my thighs were burning, I fumbled with my phone and unlocked the screen to call Shea. I wasn't sure what I expected him to do, but maybe he saw something when he left my house this morning.

"Shea," I gasped, not slowing down my pace.

"Zara, what's wrong? Are you okay?"

"No, I'm not okay. I got a note on my desk from Alan saying he knows what I did last night—"

"What?!" Shea scoffed. "That fucking bastard. He followed me this morning."

"He followed you?" I repeated, incredulous. "What do you mean?"

"This morning I noticed a dark-colored car—black, I think, but maybe navy or dark green, following me after I pulled out of your driveway. I drove like a maniac trying to lose him."

"Why didn't you tell me?"

"I was going to later," Shea snapped back. "I didn't want to worry you."

"Fucking Alan. He knows where I live. I hosted a holiday party once. And he could get my address from the employee database anyway, even if he hadn't been there. I am pretty sure he drives a black four-door Lexus."

"Yeah, it was definitely a man. He was wearing sunglasses, though."

"What am I going to do? He wants to see me in his office ASAP. I'm going to class for now, but I'll have to stop by his office after..."

"Do you want me to come with you?"

"What?!" I shrieked. "How would that help anything?"

"I'd be happy to punch him in the face for you," he offered. "You know, due to my authority issues and such."

Now it was my turn to scoff. "Yeah, I don't think that's going to solve anything. Fuck, I'm going to get denied tenure, lose my job, and I'll be teaching at some sketchy for-profit online college for ten bucks an hour before I know it."

"Go see what he wants. Do you have any leverage over him? I mean, we already know he's stalking you if he was hanging outside your house. If we can prove it, maybe we can turn the tables on him."

I racked my brain trying to think if I had any dirt on Alan. Besides his creepster ways, I couldn't think of anything. He'd rubbed me the wrong way for years, but ever since my divorce, he'd been extra creepy.

"You don't think he's...jealous, do you?" I theorized. "Of you, I mean."

"Well, of course he is, Zara. I thought that was obvious."

"Not obvious," I assured him. "I've never been that woman. Remember me in high school? Fat, nerdy and awkward?"

"Well, you blossomed," Shea reminded me. "You're fucking sexy as hell now. If you can prove that Alan is stalking you and sexually harassing you..."

"I'll see what he says."

"Record it," Shea advised. "Just start a video on your phone. It'll pick up the audio."

"I'll see what I can do."

"Call me after. I have to go to work at nine though."

"Work? What do you do?"

"Don't worry about it," he fired back. "It's only temporary."

"By the way—your second essay was a lot better."

I managed to get through my first-year English comp class lecture with no issues before marching back to the English department. I rode the elevator up to the Ivory Tower this time, preparing a speech in my head so I could get in and out of Alan's office as fast as possible. Just the thought of being alone with him sent shivers up my spine and churned my stomach. I hadn't had a bite to eat all day—and it was unlikely I'd regain my appetite anytime soon if I had to deal with him.

When I knocked on his door, a creepy-crawly feeling raised goosebumps all over my body.

"Looking for me?" came a voice from behind me. *Alan*.

"Just dropping by like you asked," I chirped as pleasantly as I could. I nodded to my colleague Ana as she passed us in the hall. Her nose wrinkled when she saw it was Alan I was talking to.

"Well, come on in." Alan unlocked the door and glanced over his shoulder at me, flashing me a lecherous grin that made him look like a gargoyle. He gestured toward the chair where I always sat when in his office, but I preferred to stay on my feet for this, my boots and hips assuming a combat-ready stance behind his desk.

"Why are you stalking me?" I asked him before he had a chance to fire off even a single word.

"Stalking you?" He threw his head back with laughter. "Why are you fucking a student? I think that's the relevant question here."

"Can you prove I'm fucking a student?" I seethed. I didn't know where this surge of badassery was coming from, but I was going to take full advantage. *Perhaps fucking your high school bully is empowering?*

"I can prove that he left your house this morning," Alan retorted, the corner of his mouth lifting in a tiny smirk. "I have it on video."

Video—speaking of which, I had my phone recording in my purse. I patted it just to make sure it was still slung over my shoulder.

"So what? He dropped by for an early morning study session. I was going over the first draft of his second essay with him," I lied. "I can forward it to you if you want. I've already put comments on it. It's about Alzheimer's disease." That part was true at least.

His eyes narrowed further. "If you were going over it in person, why did you type comments on it? Are they time-stamped?"

"So he would remember what we discussed." *Fuck.* I apparently was getting ahead of myself, and Alan was not a stupid man. I couldn't make even a single mistake, or this was going to blow up in my face.

"You know, Zara," Alan's expression shifted, his features softening, his brows arching ever so slightly, "there is a way to rectify this situation."

The way he said "rectify" made me want to retch.

"And how is that?" My heart pounded against my chest,

waiting for him to just come out and say it, what I feared he had been thinking since the day he met me.

"You know," he steepled his fingers together as his gaze swept up and down my figure, "I thought you were a good girl, Zara. First, you were married, a devoted wife. Never wanted to go out for drinks with the rest of the department and cut up on a Friday night. Even after you divorced, you were still untouchable. Pristine and pure. Never dated. Always so serious and focused on work." His eyes narrowed as he steadied his steely gray gaze on me. "But then I find out you're fucking your own student, and I realize you're not the innocent prude I thought you were. No, you're a fucking slut, Zara."

I held his gaze, not saying a word. This was exactly where I thought this would go after Shea finally confirmed what I suspected all along but was afraid to admit.

"So the real question is, do you only fuck those beneath you? Those you hold power over?" He licked his bottom lip, and it took everything within me not to throw up. "Or would you also get down and dirty with someone who holds power over you? Especially if it saved your job?"

"Are you asking me what I think you're asking me?"

His lips parted and then spread into a victorious smile. "I'll keep your secret, Zara. But I want you on your knees first. The committee meets Friday. Tomorrow night...meet me here."

He handed me a slip of paper, possibly the other half of the one he'd put on my desk this morning.

I glanced down to find an address and a time.

Eleven

Shea

I HAD JUST LEFT my afternoon class when my phone buzzed in my pocket. *Zara.* "Hey, what's going on?"

"You were right," she panted before sucking in a gasp of air.

"We need to talk in person." I might have had ulterior motives, but I really wanted to see her. If nothing else, just to make sure she was okay. She didn't *sound* okay, and it was raising my hackles.

"I don't know where. You obviously can't come to my house. Yours?"

"I can't, Zara. I already told you—"

"But why? I feel like you're hiding something from me."

"Do you want my help with this or not?" I ignored the desperate plea in her voice. Was it any of her business why she couldn't come to my house? No. We were...what were we? Fuck buddies? Teacher-student? Those were the only strings binding us together. She didn't need to know about my homelife.

"I don't know where we can go." She sounded defeated.

Where could we go to get away from this creep? "There has to be someplace on campus. Private. Discreet. Where is he right now?"

She paused for a moment like she had to look something up. "His online calendar says he has a meeting at the administration building."

It came to me like the proverbial lightbulb illuminating in my head. "The chapel on campus. There's a meditation room."

I had been there a few times when I needed to get away from everything. When I needed to clear my head of the demons fighting over possession of my last few brain cells and last bit of strength. And they always clamored for my last few fucks when I tried to reconcile what happened with my dad, with Caroline, with Mom. With getting fired from my job. The voices never fucking stopped—but they did in there. I got a respite, no matter how brief. I wasn't sure how, but I felt something in that meditation room, something I might call peace if I didn't know any better. It was a fleeting peace, I guess?

What was I saying? I would never have peace. And considering how I treated Zara when we were growing up, how I treated everyone, I probably didn't deserve it anyway.

"Meditation room, really?" She huffed out a breath. "Where in the chapel? I've never actually been inside."

"Go into the sanctuary, toward the altar, and it's the door on the right," I instructed. "I can be there in ten."

"Okay." She hung up without saying anything further.

My lungs burned as I overfilled them with the cool,

crisp air of the waning afternoon and pushed my legs to carry me across campus. The chapel was an unassuming stone building tucked back behind the student union. The windows were stained glass, and the door was recessed in a giant arch. A steeple strained toward the clouds but was dwarfed by the massive trees that ensconced the small church on every side.

There was never anyone here in the middle of the day, so this was the perfect time and place for us to rendezvous. I walked in slowly, reverently, my boots thudding on the slate tile floors as I made my way down the aisle between wooden pews. The meditation room door creaked as I pushed it open.

Zara arrived only a few minutes after I did, and though she looked frazzled, her outfit nearly made my jaw drop open. A sexy schoolgirl plaid skirt skimmed her hips, and there were only a few inches of skin between the hem and the top of black suede boots that laced all the way up her legs. *Fuck me. I'm in a house of worship, but all I want to do is worship her body.*

"What did he say?" I struggled to keep my eyes glued to her face.

"He handed me this. From what I gathered, he expects me to suck his dick." She rolled her eyes and flashed a slip of paper with an address on it. "Thursday night."

I winced knowing Judy was unable to take care of Mom that night. And I was supposed to work. I still didn't know how I was going to handle that situation.

I'd figure it out. Right now, my priority was making sure Zara was exonerated. I was pissed at her asshole boss for stalking us and for threatening to ruin her livelihood—not to mention the fact that if anything came back on me, I might not pass Zara's class, and we all knew the ramifications of that.

"I think you should meet up with him there. You recorded today's conversation, right?"

She nodded.

"Do the same this time, but instead of only recording your conversation, I want you to call me right before you go in. That way I can hear what's going on, and I'll know when to bust in on you—right before you have to actually touch the slimy weasel. I'll get it all on video too."

"Are you sure? Maybe I should just go to the campus police?" Her gaze turned down to the slip of paper before snapping back to me.

"Well, you could do that; you have the recording you made in his office to prove he's blackmailing you, right?" For some reason I was a little disappointed that she would rather do that than execute my plan, but I understood. It could be less drama. Less stress.

"Yeah." She fumbled with her phone, made a couple swipes and then held it out. "Here's what I got." The audio started to play. Her frown deepened as her voice, a higher pitch, was loud enough and clear enough to understand, but his was not. His voice was low, faint, and not intelligible.

"Fuck. It just sounds like you're confessing to fucking a student," I said when it finished playing. "You can't even hear him."

A look of resolve came over her face. "I didn't confess to fucking you. I said we had an early morning study session."

"Yeah, I'm sure the campus police are gonna buy that."

She looked up at me with pleading eyes, and all I wanted to do was make things right. Protect her.

"So...keep that note asking you to meet him. Go in all

innocent, ask him to clearly tell you what he wants you to do. Play dumb. Make him work for it. I'll come in, get the rest of it on video, and we'll have it made."

She sighed. "Alright. I just—" She looked down at the address again. "I don't even know where this is, do you?"

I took the slip from her and studied the address. "This is downtown. I think that's an office building."

"Why would he have me go there?" Her eyes locked on me, fear and trepidation radiating out. "I don't like this, Shea."

I wrapped my arms around her, pulling her close to my chest. "I'm not going to let anything bad happen to you. I promise, okay?"

A soft sniffle and sob sounded as she relaxed her head on my chest. Why did this feel so good, so right, having her here like this, holding her, protecting her, comforting her?

"You really liked me in high school?" her voice came out just above a whisper.

Her unexpected question created a lump in my throat that I swallowed down, covering it with a raspy chuckle. Her emotion was bleeding through, seeping into me. "Yes." I sucked in a whiff of her scent, filling my nostrils with it. "I still feel bad about how I handled it, especially the bullying. It's not an excuse, but I wasn't in the best place—"

"Why not?" She pulled back to look me in the eyes. "What happened?"

I pulled her back to me again so I didn't have to face her imploring stare and kissed the top of her head, stealing another lungful of her essence. "It's not important now."

"So how did you know about this room, anyway?" She lifted her head, her eyes darting around the room. The heavy blue velvet curtains were drawn, framing a small marble-topped table with candles burning. A thick rug covered the floor, topped with mounds of soft floor pillows. Everything was serene and mellow, underscored by piped-in music, a soothing pan flute over nature sounds.

"I've come here a time or two to blow off steam," I confessed. Then I realized how that sounded. "Not like that. I mean to actually meditate. Like get a mental escape from shit."

She pulled me down onto the soft pillows beneath our feet. "Sit with me a moment?" She hiked up her skirt and sat on one hip with her legs stretched out to the side, then she closed her eyes and took in a deep breath, her chest expanding as her lungs filled.

I did as she asked, sitting beside her, holding her hand. After taking one last look at her boot-covered legs and her ample hips, I closed my eyes and tried to match her breathing. *In. Out. In. Out.* The music turned to a hypnotic beat, something Middle Eastern maybe? Colors swirled behind my eyes as I imagined taking her right here in the middle of the meditation room floor.

We were in a church! A house of worship! I should not have allowed those thoughts to infiltrate my mind, but here I was, and my cock was swelling. God, everything about her was so fucking sexy. With my eyes still closed, I reached out till my fingertips grazed her thigh, then I trailed them up the curve of her hips to her chest. Her breath hitched when I reached her shoulder.

Her eyes fluttered open, and she looked at me with such hunger in her eyes, I couldn't help but inch closer to her. All I wanted to do was brush my lips against hers, and maybe that would be enough? *I can stop after that,* I convinced myself as my mouth claimed hers. But of course I wasn't satisfied with a tiny taste—I wanted to feast upon her soft wet lips.

"Shea," she breathed as I moved to her neck, her ear, down her chest to where my hands cupped her gorgeous tits and squeezed hard enough that a slight whimper escaped her throat. "Fuck, we can't—"

I shut her up with another kiss, my mouth over hers swallowing any further concerns she may have had about what we could or couldn't do. This woman looked like a goddess of lust, and I was in her temple, under her control. I couldn't be held responsible for my body's reaction to her or the way my hands and lips and cock responded to her.

With hands desperate to claim her, I hiked up her skirt, watching that few inches of exposed skin become more than a foot of luscious, creamy thighs, begging me to plunder the treasure lying between them. Even more enticing: when I discovered she wasn't wearing any panties under her sexy plaid skirt.

"Fuck, Zara, you're killing me..."

"Hurry," she gasped, surrendering to my advances. She spread her legs, bent at the knee, the laces of her boots providing leverage for my hands to spread them even further. Unbuttoning my pants and climbing into position, I steadied myself on the mound of pillows before reaching in to free my aching cock.

She choked out a desperate, "Please," as I pressed it to her lips.

"Fuck, I don't have a condom..."

"Can't get pregnant," she muttered then repeated her needy plea.

Who was I to deny her in her time of need? For once, I was yielding to authority. Parting her drenched lips, I held my breath as I worked my cock inside her, my hips pushing me home until her stolen breath hissed in her throat and her arms wrapped around me, drawing my weight on top of her.

"I want you to fuck me like you wanted to all those years ago," she seethed between clenched teeth as I took shallow strokes inside her, feeling her pussy throb around me. "How you would have if you weren't afraid of what your friends would think. What would you have done to my virgin pussy if I'd let you fuck me in your back seat after the homecoming dance twenty-five years ago?"

I groaned as my balls tightened, remembering all the times I'd jerked off thinking about her when we were growing up. I never thought in a million years I'd ever get to fuck the real Zara Fowler, or that she would turn out to be this veritable sex goddess.

So while the Middle Eastern music swirled around us, hypnotizing us with its mesmerizing beat, I drilled into her fast, hard, deep—so intense, we were both lost in our chase for release until that one pivotal moment when our eyes locked and our bodies surrendered, exploding together like twin supernovas. Exploding until there was nothing left but wilted limbs, burning lips and ragged breaths.

Then we came down together, nestled in a wondrous embrace of sated sighs and lingering pulses of pleasure.

Twelve

I WAS on edge all day. Shea and I thought it best not to interact during class, so I simply locked eyes with him and watched him nod once. The plan was still on. He was going to be on alert at the office building tonight when I went to meet Alan and burst in with the cameras rolling. He'd be listening in on the phone so he would know when.

When I arrived back at my office in the Ivory Tower, Alan was lurking in the hallway as if waiting for me to return. "Have a good class?" he schmoozed in his greasy, disingenuous voice.

"I did." I didn't even make eye contact with him, just turned my key in its lock—only to find the door was already unlocked.

"Oh, sorry about that; I forgot to lock it back." Alan shrugged. "I have a master, you know. I took the liberty of making sure there wasn't anything incriminating on your computer, you know, since we have your tenure committee meeting tomorrow."

I barely restrained myself from throwing some choice words in his direction, choosing instead to simply nod as I slipped inside. When I went to shut the door, Alan put his hand between the door and the frame, preventing me.

Though, the thought of slamming his hand in my door and pretending it was an accident did cross my mind. *So damn tempting...*

"Everything good for tonight?" His evil eyes showed the hollow passage to the dark abyss where his soul should have been. His lips twisted up into a crooked grin.

I nodded again, conserving my words. I was so fucking ready to catch this asshole and bring his treatment of me to light. How many other women in the department had he done this to through the years? He had been the departmental chair for three years, but he'd been heading up tenure committees for almost a decade.

I couldn't remember anyone being denied tenure since I'd been here, and I recalled at least eight or nine colleagues up for it—five of them, if my memory served, were female, including Ana, who'd snarled when she saw me talking to Alan in the hallway yesterday. What if he had blackmailed all of them too?

"I'll see you then," Alan promised, a metallic laugh spilling out of his thin lips. My skin crawled like I'd been tossed into a pit with thousands of bugs, worms, and millipedes. Tonight when I got home from this ordeal, I would have to scrub his slimy filth out of every pore in my body.

My plan was to work late, grading papers—the second draft of the second essay was due today—then grab a bite to eat before heading over to the address Alan had given me. I wished I was going to see Shea again before this all went down. He had such a calming effect on me—or maybe the orgasms he gave me relaxed me.

I didn't know what would happen when the semester was over, but I hoped we would still...hang out. There'd never been any talk of a relationship, but I felt we were bonding over this whole ordeal with Alan. It meant a lot to me that he was willing to help me nail the guy, especially since Shea was the one who seduced me and got me into this mess in the first place. Though I had a feeling Alan was looking for any crack in the veneer so he could worm his way in and place some draconian stipulations on my tenure approval.

Hopefully everything would work out.

Of course, I didn't have a great track record for "everything working out"—my family was toxic; my marriage had failed; I'd never been able to have children, even though I wanted them. The latter was my ex's fault. He was sterile—well, he had a low sperm count. *And, I'm no biologist, but from what I understand, you have to actually* have *sex to get pregnant.*

The one thing that had gone according to plan was my career. I carried a 4.0 all through undergrad, got into a good PhD program, and had my doctorate by the time I reached twenty-seven. Not too shabby, really. A year of post-doc work, and then I got this job. It wasn't far from home; I met Brandon at an event for a charity we were both involved in, and I thought we were going to have the American dream.

Until he cheated and was a complete asshole about it.

But I'd put all that behind me. I'd been single for three years. Before I became reacquainted with Shea, I considered putting myself back out there, maybe seeing if there were any sexy, intelligent local men worthy of my time.

And maybe I'd still do that after getting back in the groove with Shea.

You just never know.

* * *

My dinner—Thai food—sat in my stomach like a rock as I drove downtown to the office building where Alan asked me to meet him. It was nearing eight o'clock, and the city streets were empty. Stoplights turned red in sync all down the street, and I slammed on my brakes while only one or two cars crossed from the other direction. As I waited for the light to turn green, I noticed my heart rate was beginning to pick up.

Here I was being bullied again, and I was relying on my high school bully to save me. The whole thing was ridiculous, right?

My cheeks started to flush as the lunacy of it all throbbed in my head like a baby migraine feeding on my anxiety in its quest to take over my consciousness. I hadn't gotten a migraine in a while, but with the stress I was under, it was nearly inevitable.

Did I really trust Shea to swoop in and save the day when he'd ruined so much of my high school life?

Alan believed I was too scared about my reputation in the department and on campus to involve the police. He had me pegged as a weak fool, someone he could manipulate and control, a compliant pawn who would do his bidding in order to ensure I'd be granted tenure.

Shea himself favored the idea of keeping this in-house. We would use the footage to blackmail Alan right back into approving my tenure, so we didn't need law enforcement or university officials' intervention at all. We could all simply get back to our jobs—me as a professor and him as a student.

But did *I* want that?

Maybe I wanted Alan to pay for his abuse of power.

And what about me? Had I abused *my* power when I got involved with a student? Did we really have that kind of power dynamic, considering we had a history that went back more than twenty-five years?

But didn't female victims of sexual assault and harassment tend to get the tables turned on them? "Blaming the victim" was a saying for a reason.

The clock in my car glowed 7:58. I needed to make a decision and fast. Holding my breath, I picked up my phone, fired off an email I'd composed earlier and saved to drafts, and then called Shea so he could listen in on the conversation.

"Hey," came his deep voice. "Everything a go?"

"Getting ready to walk in now. Where are you?"

"I'm a block over. I'll move into position once you're inside. Did he say it was unlocked?"

"Main door is unlocked, but I don't know if Suite C will be... Is that gonna be a problem?" My voice betrayed my nerves with its wavering.

"I will kick down the goddamn door to get to you, Zara," came his reply.

The assurance and confidence in his voice sent a wave of heat through me, and the clock on my dash flicked to 8:00. "I gotta go."

"Be careful," were his last words.

I kept the call going and slipped my phone in my purse. I'd turned the volume all the way up. I really hoped there was no way the call would disconnect while I was in there. Then what would I do?

It was always helpful to have a backup plan in place...

There was a single light casting an orangish glow on the sidewalk at the entrance to the building. I tucked my chin, gritted my teeth and headed to meet my fate. This had to work. I wasn't going to let this asshole off the hook. And I sure as hell wasn't going to suck his cock.

The inside of the building was dark, each suite centered by a glass door etched with the name of the business. One was an architect; another was a lawyer. When I came to Suite C, I saw it was for a financial planner. My stomach churned as I pulled on the handle. Locked.

The doors were glass. When Shea said he was going to knock down the door... Would he really put his foot through glass for me?

I rattled the door back and forth in its frame, then heard footsteps coming from behind. My blood froze in my veins as I heard him drag in a slow breath before he spoke.

"I didn't know if you'd really show up."

I whipped around to face Alan, who was wearing a black jacket and what looked like black jeans. "Yeah, I'm here. I want my tenure."

"Aw, and here I thought maybe you genuinely liked me." His evil cackle echoed in the hallway as he pressed a card to an electronic pad outside the door. I heard it click open. Maybe it wouldn't relock?

My heart pounding erratically in my chest, and every hair on every inch of my body standing on end, I followed Alan down another hallway to an office, where he flicked on a desk lamp that filled the room with a soft yellow glow. Wall-to-wall bookcases, a window covered in blinds, and a dark wood desk with a sleek computer monitor made me wonder whose office this was. Did they have any idea what was going on in here tonight?

When he spun me to face him, I had to swallow down the bile that had pooled in the back of my throat. If I could just endure this humiliation, this utter disgustingness for a few minutes, vindication would be so sweet.

"Well, now, here we are," Alan's voice oozed with slime as he stepped closer to me. His bony fingers wrapped around my neck. "I've been waiting a long time for this, Zara. Maybe if you just relax, you'll enjoy it too?"

I sucked in a breath, my lungs burning from the stench of his heavy cologne. *I don't know if he's masking the stench of evil or what, but for fuck's sake, no one needs that much cologne.*

With his fingers still on me, he walked in a circle around me, checking me out from every angle. "You know, your lips on my cock might not be enough, now that I think about it. If you want me to vote in favor of your tenure tomorrow, my cock might need to get acquainted with your pussy—just sayin'."

My spine stiffened, and my jaw clenched so tight, it could have snapped a limb in two. Was Shea preparing to come inside? I really hoped he would get there before I had to make contact with Alan's dick—whether with my mouth or pussy.

He stopped in front of me and placed a hand on each of my shoulders. "I think you should get me nice and warmed up for the main attraction, don't you?" He shoved me down hard, forcing me to my knees.

I'd purposely worn pants today—even though I wore a skirt or a dress almost every day to work. Why make this any easier on him? Thankfully I had that layer of fabric between my knees and the thin, scratchy commercial carpet where I was perched.

He unzipped his pants. "Zara, I've been watching you for a long time. How long have you been here, eight years? Ten? I guess if I'd bothered to read your tenure dossier, I'd know, wouldn't I?" A sardonic laugh spilled out of his throat as he threw his head back and his hand gripped his cock inside his underwear.

"You've always been beautiful, but something about you—it seems like you have ripened with age. All I can think about is those pretty red lips wrapped around my cock, and then my cock driving in and out of your pretty pink pussy. Feel what you do to me."

He leaned down and sucked in a whiff of me, closing his eyes as he savored my scent. *Ewww.* I started to recite lines of poetry in my head, hoping it would drown out his words, his smell, his hot breath hissing out as he circled me like I was his prey.

Once upon a midnight dreary, while I pondered, weak and weary,

Over many a quaint and curious volume of forgotten lore,

While I nodded, nearly napping, suddenly there came a tapping,

As of some one gently rapping, rapping at my chamber door.

"It's such a shame I don't have anything else over you," he rambled on while more lines of The Raven echoed in my mind. "This may only be a one-time thing, but I'm hoping you like it so much—you little fucking whore—you'll come back for more. You're definitely on the hefty side, which means your relationship prospects are probably slim." He burst into a grating maniacal chuckle, and the migraine that was brewing earlier roared to life again inside my skull, making me lose my spot in Poe's masterpiece.

He slapped his knee, he was so amused by his ridiculous pun. "'Slim'! See what I did there? But I don't care about that, Zara. I think every inch of you is juicy and fuckable."

I bit my lip to keep myself from blurting out my

thoughts on that sentiment. Could I escape into another poem? *Dickinson, perhaps? No—Plath.*

Then he gripped my hand, jerking it up from my side, and placed it on the bulge in his underwear, which felt damp. I struggled not to retch; this was so disgusting. My purse was on the desk. I really hoped it was still transmitting our conversation to Shea.

"Do you feel what you do to me?" He pulled out his gnarly cock, which was thin, stubby and covered in long, dark, crinkly pubic hair. Quite frankly, it was the nastiest penis I had ever seen—not that I'd seen that many.

"You're disgusting," I spat at him, praying Shea would burst in at any moment.

"Oh, I'm sorry, did you want me to woo you with a poem first?" He laughed again when my jaw clenched even tighter. "Look, you fat slut, do you want tenure or not?" he growled low in his throat as he took the tip of his cock and rubbed it against my lips.

On the verge of losing my dinner, I shouted, "Help!" hoping that would send Shea inside.

"Stop screaming, you fucking bitch!" His hands went right for my throat. "You agreed to do this, so it's time to pony up!"

Knowing I probably outweighed him by a good forty or fifty pounds, I forced my way to standing, gripping his thin wrists and using them for leverage. I wasn't about to let him take advantage of me. Shea promised he would bust in before anything actually happened. *Where the fuck is he?*

Alan and I wrestled next to the desk, and as I shoved him hard, his outstretched arm knocked my purse off the desk. My phone tumbled across the floor, landing right at Alan's feet. The screen displayed my ongoing phone call with Shea, but it said I'd been on hold for two minutes.

What the fuck is he doing? Talking to someone else?

"You're recording this?" Alan seized my phone between his bony fingers and looked at me with fury blazing in his eyes. "Fuck you, Zara." He dropped the phone to the floor and stomped on it with his foot.

My heart sank. There went my evidence. My breath ragged, my entire body shaking with adrenaline, I locked gazes with Alan, trying to figure out my next move.

"Now!" he demanded, his determination renewed. "You don't wanna suck my cock? Fine, I'll just fuck you instead." He dove for my legs, knocking me off-balance and back to the floor. I hit my head on the edge of the desk, but I barely felt the pain due to the anger flowing like venom through my veins.

When Alan tried to wrestle me onto my back, I stuck my neck out, made contact with his shoulder, and clamped my teeth down hard, right in the muscle. Howling in pain, he pried my mouth off him and punched me in the nose. Even with blood gushing out of both nostrils, I didn't hesitate to lift my legs and kick him off with me with every bit of force I could muster, sending him flying backwards.

That was when my backup plan kicked in.

Sirens screamed in the distance, moving toward us fast.

Alan took a final slit-eyed look at me and fled, leaving me in a pool of my own blood with my smashed phone beside me.

Thirteen

Shea

IT TOOK every ounce of restraint in my body to let Zara walk inside that building. If I came face to face with this asshole boss of hers, I'd probably punch his lights out. I grunted when I realized that could become a self-fulfilling prophecy in a matter of minutes.

"I gotta go," she said, her words full of resolve.

"Be careful," I replied before putting the phone on speaker. Watching her walk up to the building and pull open the door, I lifted up a silent prayer that the timing on this would work perfectly. Alan was about to get a taste of his own medicine.

I closed my eyes, listening to each word they said, tuning in to the ambient noises: feet shuffling across the carpet, a soft thud, a zipper? My eyes flew open when the sound seemed to be interrupted.

I was getting another call.

Fuck!

I went to press decline when I noticed the caller was "Judith Norris."

It was my neighbor Judy, who took care of my mother. Only she just had surgery, and her daughter was supposed to be staying with her. What if something had happened to her? Or Mom?

Fuck.

I clicked over—I would call them back if it wasn't an emergency, but I had to know. I'd rush in as soon as I knew for certain—whether or not I got a signal from Zara. I'd already recorded quite a bit of the conversation, and it didn't look good for Alan, even if he hadn't gotten to the actual point of assaulting her.

"Hey," I panted, "what's wrong?"

"The police are looking for you," came a soft female voice. "This is Shea Hunt, right? Pat Hunt's son?"

"What happened?" I rushed out, wishing I could speed up the time of this call and slow down time in the office building all at once.

"Your mother—they just took her to the ER via ambulance. I don't know what happened, just that the police are looking for you. My mother asked me to call you and let you know. She just gave them your number; she's talking to them now."

Fuck. Another call came through just then, and I realized when I looked at my phone screen that the call from Zara had disconnected. The new caller was listed as Emergency Services.

"Thanks, they're calling now." My head fell into my hand as I switched over. "This is Shea Hunt."

Zara

Everything was hazy, my head throbbing as paramedics surrounded me. The sound of muted voices being transmitted over the police radio echoed in my ears. "Ouch! Careful!" I snapped as they lifted me onto a stretcher and began to wheel me out of the building.

Red and blue lights bounced off the building and reflected in the glass doors as they rushed me toward what I could only assume was an ambulance. Facing toward the building, I couldn't see where they were taking me. When I looked up, the stern face of a female police officer was staring down at me, her dark, smooth skin shining in the swirling lights.

"Can I get your name and date of birth?" she asked.

I rattled it off as quickly as I could, despite my head feeling like it was going to explode.

"Do you know who did this to you?" she asked, but her voice became muffled as paramedics put an IV in my hand.

The only word I could get out of my mouth as they pushed the gurney into the waiting rig was, "Shea..."

Shea

I made another phone call on my way to the hospital, then slammed on the brakes and whipped into a parking space in the visitor lot outside the ER. My thighs and lungs burned in the cool night air as I bolted inside the building, stopping at the counter inside to give my name and show my ID. The smiling receptionist directed me toward a bank of chairs facing the double doors that led to the patient bays.

I whipped out my phone and called Zara's number again, but it went straight to voicemail. *What does that mean? What happened to her?* I prayed she was okay.

I had to make a split-second decision—my seventy-year-old mother with Alzheimer's versus a healthy forty-two-year-old who was up against, yes, a monster, but one who was, as far as I could tell, unarmed. I knew, ultimately, Zara could handle herself. She didn't need me fighting her battles on her behalf, but I accidentally got her in over her head when I seduced her in her office. Guilt and my need to protect her combined, compelling me to help her turn the tables on her abusive boss.

Yet I had a feeling, even if I hadn't gotten involved with her, he would have figured out some way to blackmail her. And I had a feeling, based on the conversation I heard, it wasn't the first time he'd done this, the creepy fucking bastard.

Before I could try to call her phone again, a doctor and a police officer appeared at the double doors, calling my name and ushering me back. It felt like it was happening in slow motion, my feet like concrete blocks as I trudged down the hallway to the room they were guiding me to.

When I stepped inside, my eyes watered at the strong smell of antiseptic. My mother was hooked to all kinds of wires and tubes, and the monitors were softly pinging with readings. "Is she okay?"

"This is your mother? Patricia Hunt?" the doctor clarified. I watched the police officer, a burly white man with a five o'clock shadow, take notes.

I nodded. "What happened?"

"She activated the emergency button she wears," the cop explained, "and when we arrived, she was unresponsive. We suspect she took some medications, then fell and could not get back up. The doctors are running some tests to see what substances she took."

"Do you have a list of medications she's on?" the doctor, a petite woman with sable skin and matching hair, asked.

"Yes, just a moment." I shoved my hand in my pocket to retrieve my phone. I had taken a photo of her prescriptions and dosages for this exact situation, if it ever arose.

But I should have been with her. I would have given her the correct medications and helped get her into bed before I went to work. This wouldn't have happened if I'd been home.

Just like twenty-five years ago when something tragic happened because I failed to put my family first.

Zara

The ambulance ride was a blur. Lights, sirens, scenery whizzing by with the streetlights and stoplights looking like big snowflakes. *They must have taken my contacts out—only my astigmatism could make the lights spread out in lacy patterns like that.* And when we got to the hospital, it was a crash to the ground, cool wind on my face around the oxygen mask, and then bright fluorescent lights blinding me as they wheeled me down a long hallway and made a sharp turn to the right.

I could have sworn we passed a room where a man who

reminded me of Shea—same build, same salt and pepper hair—perched beside the bed of a patient connected to tubes and wires and monitors. Surely my head injury and the drugs being pumped through my IV were making me hallucinate.

"Where's my phone?" I murmured as the gurney came to rest in an exam room. A doctor appeared in blue scrubs with purple gloves on her hands.

"Ms. Ames?" I heard through her mask.

"Dr. Ames," I corrected her. *I must not be too out of it.*

"I'm sorry, Dr. Ames. Do you want to tell me what happened? Are you in pain?"

"I need my phone and my glasses," I snapped back, becoming agitated. Being in this bed was bad enough, but not being able to see was infuriating.

A nurse patted my hand, his large palm spreading over my smaller one. "Is there someone we can call for you? A partner? Parent? Child? Friend?"

I shook my head. *Nope, I'm a lone wolf,* I wanted to say, but I bit my lip instead as the doctor began to examine me. "I met up with my boss in that office building," I began, struggling against her roaming hands. I wasn't about to lie, not when I had proof of what happened.

Or did I?

What the hell happened to Shea?

He's the one with the proof...

When I jerked away from her, the doctor mumbled something to the nurse. A coldness seeped through my IV, making my body shudder, then still.

As I lay there claiming I didn't remember what happened exactly, but I suspected my boss assaulted me, not being able to see, and the symphony of low voices, the beeps and blips all muddled together forced a disassociation.

Suddenly I was on the ceiling looking down at myself being examined by two doctors and a nurse.

They were asking me questions, whether or not I felt pain in my limbs, in my abdomen, and Bed Me murmured "yes" or "no." But Floating Me spun away, recessing into a memory that was deeply submerged in my psyche.

Homecoming dance—senior year.

I think it's Nirvana playing. The DJ is set up on the stage in the gym, the one where I performed the role of Cousin Cora in Life with Father *my freshman year. Lights are flashing, swirling—not just red and blue, like earlier tonight, but pink and purple and teal and yellow and green. My head is spinning as I look around and see everyone in semi-formal attire. The girls are wearing short sequined dresses that are sleeveless or have spaghetti straps, and the boys are wearing shirts and ties.*

My arms are too fat—I need sleeves to hide them—so I'm wearing a long-sleeve knee-length emerald-green velvet dress that is stretchy but fitted in the bodice and flares at the hip. I'm fairly certain no one has looked at me except my two best friends, Jenny Birt and Katie Hitchcock.

Bed Me wonders where Jenny and Katie ended up...

Back to Floating Me, I've embodied this velvet dress, and I'm trying to dance, my limbs flailing, and Bed Me realizes how lucky I am that social media wasn't a thing in the nineties, or my dancing would have certainly become a viral video or a meme of some sort.

Bed Me is thinking what the hell kind of drugs did they give me?

Katie dances over to me. "They're going to announce the homecoming king and queen and their court soon." She looks all googly-eyed because she has a crush on Dalton Thomas, who is up for homecoming prince in the junior class and is also in her psychology class. However, I am pretty sure he doesn't have a clue she even exists.

"Who'll be crowned king?" Jenny hovers close to us.

"Duh! It will be Shea Hunt for sure!" Katie rolls her eyes.

Velvet-clad Floating Me freezes. Shea Hunt, who had jokingly asked me to be his date for this dance. I'm going to have to watch him wear the homecoming king crown and dance with some girl—probably Amanda Franklin. Could I leave? Damn it, I'm stuck here until my parents pick me up at eleven.

Bed Me is lamenting the lack of cell phones in my youth.

"There goes the assistant principal!" Jenny shrieks, grabbing my hand and squeezing.

Mrs. Pastorelli awkwardly takes the microphone from the DJ, who was seated, and instead of picking it up off the stand or adjusting it, she just bends down to speak into it. "Good evening, everyone! Thank you for coming, and thank you for supporting the Eagles football team. Even though we didn't win tonight, we're proud of the way our boys played, aren't we, Eagles?"

Everyone musters a clap, but when Mrs. Pastorelli applauds loudly right next to the microphone—after all, it is at the same height as her hands—it sounds like we're in a war zone or something. The DJ is looking at her like she has two heads, so that's pretty entertaining.

She shuffles some cards in her hand and looks out across the sea of teenage faces—we probably look like something out of the Nirvana "Smells Like Teen Spirit" video, to be honest. "I have the names of the king, queen, and other members of the homecoming court. Does anyone want to know who they are?"

Everyone cheers. I think Katie's piercing scream has burst my eardrum, in fact. Mrs. Pastorelli rushes through the underclass prince and princesses, because, frankly, who cares about them, anyway?

Bed Me is amused by this memory, apparently. Just as the blood pressure cuff starts to squeeze the ever-loving shit out of my arm.

"And now for the moment we've all been waiting for!" she continues. "This is interesting..." She stares down at the card in her hand. "I don't know if we've ever had this happen before, but a write-in candidate has received more votes than the four ladies who were previously nominated for homecoming queen."

I'm watching Jenny and Katie, who are straining to see over some taller boys and their dates. The guy in front of us has his hand planted directly on the girl's ass.

Bed Me feels compelled to roll my eyes at that.

There's a sudden wallop across my back. "Oh my god, Zara, that's you! You won!" Jenny screams in my ear.

I turn to face her, my eyes narrowed, struggling to understand the words coming out of her mouth.

Katie now: "Go! Go up there and get your crown! Oh my gosh! This is so exciting!"

As I start to stumble toward the stage, I notice a few snickers from the sea of my classmates, and Mrs. Pastorelli announces, "And this year's homecoming king is... Drumroll, please... Shea Hunt!"

Everyone is cheering and laughing, and I find myself standing next to the stage with the rest of the homecoming court. Then a loud hubbub of whispers and snickers and finger-pointing all happens at once, the sound swirling around me, eyes flashing to me and then quickly away. I hear bits and pieces of conversation around me; even the underclassmen seem to know what's going on.

"Shea isn't here," someone tells me to my face, and then he bursts into laughter.

A woman jumps up on the stage and takes the microphone. "Sorry, everyone. Shea Hunt couldn't be here tonight." That was the gym teacher. She's married to the basketball coach. Shea's basketball coach.

Mrs. Pastorelli nods and forces a smile. "Let's snap a quick photo of everyone in their crowns, and then we'll have our royal dance."

Shea isn't here?

How did I get chosen?

People wrote in my name?

This was a joke, wasn't it?

It all became clear to Bed Me as Floating Me snapped into nothingness right before my eyes. Both versions of me converged into one in the hospital bed, where the beeps and blips slowly faded into my consciousness again. But this time I was alone.

They were making fun of me. Shea got word of it ahead of time and decided not to show up, so he didn't have to be part of the joke. His friends were teasing him for giving me a hard time about the dance, and instead of facing the music, he just stayed home. Or maybe he was in on it too, who knows? Was this what he was apologizing for the other night? Was this why he was so surprised I forgave him?

I had totally blocked out that memory. Completely covered it over like it was buried in concrete, never to see the light of day. But now it had all come crashing down on me. I'd bolted just moments before "the royal dance," tossing my crown to the floor behind me. I made it halfway home in the cool October night before my parents found me on their way to pick me up.

A monitor made a loud pinging sound, and Bed Me started shaking. The nurses rushed in and covered me with a warm blanket as the female cop hovered over me, asking if I was okay.

But I wasn't okay.

And I didn't know if I ever would be.

Shea Hunt had betrayed me again.

Fourteen

Shea

EVERY TIME I tried to call Zara's phone, it went directly to voicemail. I was sure she'd blocked my number. They were keeping my mother for observation overnight, waiting for some test results and a consult with a cardiologist because there was some abnormality detected in one of the many, many tests they ran.

I'd been fighting with doctors, nurses, insurance companies, Medicare, and God knows who else for so many years now, it was a wonder I'd even been able to keep a job. That was what I told my boss when she called wondering where the hell I'd been.

"You're a good security guard, Shea, but if you don't get your act together, I won't hesitate to fire you," she told me. She wasn't the type to mince words, which I ordinarily preferred and appreciated, but it was hard to hear when it was about me letting her down.

"I don't know what to say except I'm sorry. Her paid caretaker had surgery this week, and I'm the only other person who can take care of her. I left her alone long enough to go to the store last night, and she ended up in the ER. What am I supposed to do?"

My boss's voice softened, "I understand, but I'm trying to run a business here."

I understood. Lord, I understood. And I hadn't lied to her except for the one night I'd spent at Zara's. I supposed it *was* my fault. If I hadn't done that, then her boss wouldn't have caught us, and he wouldn't have blackmailed her, and she wouldn't have been at that office building tonight. I just needed to know what happened to her.

I replayed her phone conversation with that fucking asshole, which I recorded with an app. It left off when I got the first call from the police. Apparently when they called while I was already on the phone with Judy's daughter, my call with Zara disconnected. I prayed I had enough recorded to get that fucker fired, but I needed to make sure she wanted to stick with the original plan to blackmail him right back and keep the police and the higher-ups at the university out of it.

I was so angry at what happened, I wanted to go to the police myself, but I'd wait to talk to her. I didn't want to make the situation worse. I'd certainly done that in the past —like the homecoming dance.

I had a good excuse for that, though.

Just like I did this time.

God, my family always managed to fuck me over.

Zara

I looked at myself in the mirror, examining my black eye and swollen nose from where Alan punched me. It did take me a few minutes to piece together what happened, after the drugs wore off, after Floating Seventeen-Year-Old Me seemed to be gone for good. *Thank God.* I never wanted to see her again.

I wondered if Shea recorded the phone conversation like he promised. And why he didn't show up. Just like he didn't show up that night at the homecoming dance.

After stopping by to pick up a new phone—*more answers to prayer: mine was insured*—I headed to campus, dark sunglasses covering my bruises. I rushed into the elevator without having to speak to anyone. My stomach lurched as the car carried me up to the Ivory Tower and spit me out into the cold, sterile environment of the English Department.

The clock above the administrative assistant's desk said 8:30. My tenure committee was meeting at ten o'clock. If our plan had gone off without a hitch, Shea and I would have confronted Alan with the audio from our encounter and threatened to go to the police if he didn't approve my tenure.

But now that plan had been ruined. Shea fled the scene, and though I told the police what happened, gave a formal statement once my head stopped pounding and allowed me to process language again, they didn't tell me they were planning to arrest Alan. They didn't say much about him at all, in fact.

I suppose a forty-something-year-old woman found in a pool of her own blood in an empty office building down-town at night without a soul around did seem pretty suspicious. And for me to claim my boss—who had nothing to do with the office building—is the one who assaulted me was even crazier.

But he had to have gotten that key somewhere.

Right?

I settled myself at my desk and started to look through my notes for today's intensive writing seminar. Ordinarily we had class on Tuesdays, Thursdays and Fridays. Tuesdays and Thursdays were the lecture days, and Friday was the discussion period. I generally gave them Fridays to work on their research or essays, but today—

Shit. I was supposed to finish grading their last essays, and I didn't get around to it the night before. *Something about spending several hours in the ER and being hopped up on pain meds isn't conducive to grading papers.*

I pulled up Shea's paper, hoping he hadn't implemented the changes from his last draft so I could put a big fat F on the paper and be done with it. He was going to fail my class, just like he failed me.

Why did I hallucinate he was at the hospital last night?

You couldn't see, Zara, remember? You're blind as a bat without your glasses.

I'm obsessed with this dude, aren't I?

Why does he have to have such an amazing cock?

And give breath-stealing kisses?

And have toe-curling oral skills?

Fuck.

I began to skim his paper, making a few grammatical corrections with my red pen. But then as I kept reading, I was entranced. His paper was concise, informative, and actually made me interested in learning more about Alzheimer's research for myself.

That's weird. His last paper was on Alzheimer's and

experimental drugs, and this one is on Alzheimer's research.
Why is he so obsessed with it?

Why am I so obsessed with him?

Shea

I told the doctors I couldn't come back to pick Mom up until four. I needed to go to class. I needed to see her. "Call me if there are any changes, or if it's an emergency," I relayed to the nurse as I was walking out to my truck so I could drive to campus.

The whole walk from the parking lot to the building where my English class was, I both dreaded and looked forward to seeing Zara. I would have to hope she would stay after class and speak to me. I knew she wasn't going to give anything away during class in front of her other students. She would also be handing back the first draft of our third essay, so I was anxious to see what kind of feedback she'd given me. I tried to incorporate all the suggestions she made on my first two essays into my third.

I got to class early since I didn't work last night, and I didn't have to cook breakfast for Mom. I sat in the back and watched the other students filter in, and then finally our professor. She was dressed in all black today, black pencil skirt with a black polka-dot blouse that tied at the neck, and a black cardigan over it, black boots on her feet. She even wore black sunglasses.

"Dr. Ames? Are you alright?" asked a brownnosing redhead in the front row.

"I'm fine, sorry. My eyes are sensitive due to a medication I'm taking," she explained, her voice sounding as strong and commanding as ever. "I'm hoping the sensitivity will improve with time."

"Okay," the girl said like she was sorry she asked.

Zara started up the computer on the instructor's station and opened her lecture notes on the screen. Fridays, we usually had time to work on our assignments, but it looked like we were getting a talking-to today. Our third essay drafts must not have impressed her much.

"We're going to go over Worked Cited pages again today because I've noticed you're still having some issues getting the formatting correct. I'm going to show you some examples, and then you're going to team up with a partner to tackle a worksheet with various types of sources." She rubbed her temple for a moment like she was fighting off a headache. "Oh, and I'm sorry to say that I didn't get your third essay drafts graded due to unforeseen circumstances last night. But I will get them to you before the end of the weekend; I promise. I'll give you an extra two days to work on the next draft. So that means they'll be due right before Fall Break."

Everyone groaned before she focused the class's attention on her citation examples. I watched her move stiffly to the screen to point out the different parts: the author, title, publisher, date, page numbers. She looked as though she was hurting, and it made me want to stop class, take her into my arms, and look her over from head to toe to uncover the source of her pain. I wanted to take it away. It was making me hurt to look at her.

As soon as class was over, I waited impatiently while everyone ambled out but not nearly fast enough for my taste. Zara was packing up her things and about to follow the last student out the door when I cleared my throat. "Can I have a moment?"

She slowly spun to face me. "I don't really want to speak with you, Mr. Hunt." She lowered her sunglasses and revealed her black eye before adjusting them back in place. This close to her now, I could also see she was wearing a lot of makeup on her nose—it looked swollen.

"Zara, please, give me a chance to explain what happened." I looked down at my hands and saw there was still a visitors bracelet on my wrist from the hospital. How had I managed to overlook that when I showered and changed clothes this morning? I guessed it was because my head felt like mush, and I hadn't had coffee yet. I hooked my finger in it near where it fastened and gave it a good jerk.

"What's that?" Zara's brows rose as her eyes snapped to the paper bracelet in my hand that was stamped with the hospital logo and VISITOR in bold letters.

"Oh, this is the reason I had to bail last night." I waved the bracelet and shook my head. "My mom went to the ER. I got the call after you'd been in there with your boss for only a few minutes. I'm so fucking sorry, Zara. She took the wrong medication and fell—"

Her brows knit as she stared at me. "Does your mother happen to have Alzheimer's?"

My spine stiffened as I rose to my full height. "Yeah, guess it was obvious from my papers..."

She let out a sigh. "I don't know how I knew beforehand, but I was afraid you wouldn't come through last night. So I emailed the police's Tip Line to give them an anonymous heads-up that something was about to go down at that office building. They came just in time—before I really had to pay the piper, so to speak. But at least they showed up, and Alan ran away like the little coward he is. Not before he punched me, though."

"Fucking bastard!"

Another sigh escaped her mouth as her chin tilted, and she raised her sunglasses to look at the clock on the wall. "It's ten-thirty. My tenure committee meeting should be over soon. I suppose he showed up like nothing ever happened..."

"I wouldn't be too sure about that," I said. "C'mon. I'll walk you back to your office."

She said nothing this time, just gathered up her things and followed me down the hall to the elevator, which we rode in silence. I wanted to reach out and touch her, hold her, comfort her. I felt like a pile of shit that I couldn't help her.

How did I keep hurting this woman? First in high school and now this?

I wasn't worthy of her.

Even though I desperately wanted to be.

Fifteen

Zara

LEAVES WERE CHANGING color on campus, creating a vibrant backdrop for our walk across the quad to the language arts building where my office was. So many feelings were swirling around inside me—my insides looked like all those leaves, being tossed about on autumnal winds. Shea's reason for abandoning me last night seemed legit. I wanted to ask him a million questions—*is your mother the reason you don't want me at your house?* But we walked in silence.

From looking at my watch, I knew my tenure meeting was likely over. I did have an acquaintance on the committee, fellow English professor Laura Stanley. I could ask her what was said.

Last night, I'd given the police my story, and if they didn't want to pursue a criminal investigation, then I would go to my dean and tell her what happened with Alan. I would likely face disciplinary measures or even termination for my relationship with Shea, but at least I could stop Alan from doing this again. Or I hoped to, anyway.

"Wait…" I stopped midstride, jerking to a halt as I watched two campus police officers escorting a man from the language arts building. I squinted—it looked like Alan?

When I turned to Shea, his face was beaming uncontrollably. "I told you not to count on it."

My jaw dropped as I stared at him, lips parted. "Did you have something to do with this?"

He shrugged but couldn't hide his grin. "Maybe?"

I didn't want to make a scene here on the sidewalk in the middle of the quad with hundreds of students milling about between classes. There was already a small crowd gathered near the entrance to the building where a campus police cruiser was parked at the curb. Everyone was intent on watching the chair of the English department being escorted to the cruiser and placed into the back seat. Gritting my teeth, I marched toward the building, preparing in my mind the list of questions I had for Shea as soon as we had a moment's privacy.

But before we got to the front doors, my phone buzzed in my purse. I quickly discovered it was the city police. I held my breath as I pressed the green button to accept the call. "Hello?"

"Dr. Ames? This is Detective Rebecca Rollins—we spoke at the hospital? I need you to come to the station for some follow-up questions after your attack last night. When are you available?"

"Hi, yes. I just need to grab a few things from my office, and I can be right there," I stammered, eyes bouncing between Shea, the police cruiser as it drove off, and the crowd beginning to disperse as we crossed the street out front to get to the main entrance.

"Great. Just ask for me at the front desk. See you soon."

After disconnecting, I jogged up the concrete steps to the front door, and Shea ran ahead to chivalrously swing the door open for me. I barely made it three steps before Laura Stanley, my departmental colleague, plus two other committee members blocked my path.

"What happened, Zara?" Laura looked like she was nearly ready to burst, her pale skin reddening as the words flew out of her mouth. "We were sitting in your tenure meeting, going over your dossier when two campus police officers stormed in and confronted Alan."

"I, uh..." I glanced around, looking to see who was in the vicinity. I wasn't sure it was a good idea to give any details. Right now, Alan was at the police station telling them I had an inappropriate relationship with a student. Not that doing so was in any way, shape, or form as bad as what he did to me.

But I was sure he would try to paint me as some sort of harlot who encouraged his advances. Maybe he was turning it around to say *I* was offering *him* bribes to approve my dossier...

"Zara, we voted without him—all unanimously approving your tenure. You've done some great work, especially your innovative peer-review process, not to mention the—" another committee member said, but his words were lost to the jumble in my mind as I prepared myself for what might happen when I arrived to speak with Detective Rollins.

"Zara, did you hear what I said? You got tenure. The dean and president still have to approve, but it's through the committee! Congratulations!" Laura clapped me on the back.

"Thanks, everyone. Sorry, I have to run." I forced a grin and hit the elevator up button while Shea stood guard at my side. Everything was too much right now. My lungs felt like they might explode, and my heart would be right behind them.

There was no way the dean and president were going to approve my tenure when Alan told them what I did with Shea. This was far from over.

Shea

Zara seemed shellshocked as we made our way onto the elevator and rode to her floor. I followed her down the hallway to her office, which she unlocked. Alan's door at the end of the hallway was closed, but the glass window showed the lights were off. Thank God he was gone. I hoped he wouldn't be coming back.

"What do you need? Do you want me to come too? I can drive you if you'd like," I offered as she stood looking around her office in a daze. Unfortunately I was all too familiar with that look, having seen it on my mother's face when she first became ill. Now she was a hollow body with no one inside except when painful memories from years ago haunted her—memories no one should ever have to relive.

"I'm fine," Zara muttered as she sat at her desk and made a few clicks with her computer. "I just—oh, the phone call. I don't know when we got cut off. Is it all erased?"

A wide smile spread across my face. "No, Zara."

"Why are you looking at me like that?" Her dark brows arched as she studied my face, searching for answers.

"The evidence I recorded was dropped off at the campus police station this morning anonymously."

"What?!" Her eyes widened. "You? You gave them—"

"Anonymously," I corrected her. "With a note saying who the two parties speaking were. Also, in case you're wondering, it's Alan's brother who is the financial planner, the one whose office you were in last night. Once they match Alan's voice to the tape and show he got the key from his brother..."

"Wow." She shook her head. But then a tiny frown curled the edges of her lips.

"What?" I already felt shitty about what happened to her the night before. I couldn't protect her—I should have been there. I should have kept her from getting hurt. I had probably failed her in some other way too.

"But once he tells them about my relationship with you, the dean and university president won't sign off on my tenure," she explained. "I'm going to be right back at square one, and he knows it."

"So we just deny it!"

She looked at me, still shaking her head. "Everyone just saw you walking me across campus. Everyone saw you follow me in here."

"I'm your student. We were discussing my paper." I shrugged. There had to be an answer to every accusation. We didn't come this far for her not to get tenure.

She stood up and smoothed her black skirt. "I need to get to the police."

"Right." I understood what she was getting at. The only way this was going to work was if we painted Alan as a liar, claimed to have no relationship, and we stayed away from each other, rising above suspicion for the rest of the semester.

It was for the best, really. I had my mother to take care of. I needed to buckle down and pass Zara's class, keep my grades up, get into business school. I needed to go to work, get my four to five hours of sleep, and keep everything going. I needed to man the fuck up, which meant not fucking around with my beautiful English professor.

Easy come, easy go.

It's just sex, right?

Then why did I miss the fuck out of her before I even left her office?

Zara

I stood by my office door watching Shea Hunt walk down the hall, back to the main hallway of the building. Right before he disappeared, he looked over his shoulder at me, casting me this look that I might spend the rest of my life trying to interpret. It seemed to be a mixture of regret, hope, and...something softer...affection? Longing?

Standing there, that last look embossing itself on my memory, I felt a tap on my arm. I startled, looking down to see my colleague Ana Lopez peering up at me from her petite four-foot-eleven frame with wide brown eyes.

"Can we talk for a moment?" She looked over her shoulder to make sure no one else was in the hallway.

I nodded. "What's up?"

"I need to tell you what happened two years ago when I was up for tenure... Close the door."

From the look on her face, which was pinched in an anxious way, I could tell this was serious. Ana was typically the "class clown" of our department. She was a tiny little thing with a wicked fast tongue, always prepared with a comeback for any situation. We weren't really friends, but we were friendly.

I gestured toward the chair by my desk and shut the door before returning to my own chair behind the desk. "What is it?"

Ana took a deep breath and leveled her gaze on me. I could tell this was taking every ounce of courage she had to spit out: "Alan blackmailed me for his approval on my tenure application."

My heart thundered inside my chest as the queasiness I had last night suddenly returned full force. "What did he do?"

"He told me if I didn't let him touch me, he'd vote no on my tenure bid. He wanted to touch my breasts while he jerked off..." Her voice drifted off in a way that let me know she went through with it; the mortification was carved into her features as her gaze fell to her hands.

"Oh, Ana..." My hands went to my mouth, covering up my combination of a gasp and a sigh. I had a feeling that was where she was going. "We have to stop him. Oust him. Punish him—for all he's done."

"I couldn't go forward," she said, voice quivering, "because that was when Ed Whipple was Dean and Max Buchanan was President. It was a good ol' boys club back then. They never would have believed me. They probably would've said I was harassing him by wearing short skirts or something."

I huffed out a disgusted scoff because she was so right about that.

Now she met my gaze, and it was blazing with steely determination. "If he did something like that to you, and you're going to report him, I want to go too."

"I'm going to the police right now," I explained. "I have proof. And your story will only corroborate mine. Will you come with me?"

Maybe even if I didn't get tenure because of my relationship with Shea—which I planned to deny, deny, deny—I could at least make Alan pay for what he'd done to me and Ana—and probably more women in our department as well.

"I will," she said. "I just finished my last class of the day, so I'm all yours."

"Let's do this."

Sixteen

Shea

WHEN I PICKED my mother up at the hospital, she was sedated. She didn't know who I was—that was no surprise, of course. The nurses were all kind and gentle with her, and clearly sympathetic toward me.

One young nurse wore her hair in a long auburn ponytail that swung when she walked. "Do you have any questions before we help you load her into your truck?" I had a little stool that she could step onto, which helped, but I usually had to hoist her in from the other side. At least she was light.

"No, I've been doing this a while," I confirmed, giving the nurse a small smile.

"I'm Amber," she said. "Here, I wrote down my number in case you need anything." She handed me a little card—looked like a coupon for some prescription medication—and there was a number written in blue ink on the back. She smiled, her eyes flitting down to the card and then back to mine. "Really, call me anytime. Even just to talk."

Her smile was bright, her eyes full of concern and—interest in me, if I wasn't mistaken. It would be so easy to call Amber, ask her to come over to take care of Mom, take care of me.

I thanked her, dipping my chin as a second nurse appeared. She was older, at least a decade older than me, with well-worn frown lines around her mouth. "Ready to go?"

I nodded. I wouldn't be calling Amber. She was cute, and she seemed friendly, but she just didn't capture my attention that way.

I was afraid that was because only one woman had captured me "that way" in a long while, and even though I couldn't be around her, I didn't think I would be able to break the spell she'd cast over me.

The nurses wheeled my mother down the hallway to the elevator, while I took the stairs to retrieve my truck and pull it around to the covered awning. It took all three of us to get my mother situated in the passenger seat, and I thanked the nurses for their help. Amber winked at me as if to say she hoped to hear from me soon.

I wasn't more than a block or two from the hospital when my mother groaned. Then she mumbled, "Where's Caroline?"

I put my hand on my mother's leg and patted her gently. "Mom, Caroline isn't here anymore."

"Caroline's dead," my mother whispered.

"Yes, Mama." I swallowed hard. The days she remembered her daughter was gone were the worst days. It was much easier when it remained forgotten.

"Why?" She drew in a deep, long breath before letting it

out in an anguished wail. "Why did you let it happen? Why did you let her die?"

She shook with anger and grief, her face reddening as I tried to concentrate on the road. "Mama, it wasn't me," I told her.

But wasn't it?

If I hadn't stayed after school that day to work on the homecoming float. If I had just gone to pick my sister up when I was supposed to.

"Where's Michael? Michael always knows what to do..."

"Ma, you know Dad's gone too." I patted her leg again as we pulled into our driveway. The gray siding on the house looked grayer and drabber than ever. The windows seemed to be opaque instead of clear. Everything looked so depressing, I dreaded going inside.

But this is my life, I reminded myself. *It's what I deserve.*

As I settled my mother in her armchair, a little spark of a thought raced through my head. What if, in high school, I'd pursued Zara Fowler because I thought she was smart and pretty and didn't give a fuck what my friends thought?

What if we'd gone to homecoming that night and actually been crowned king and queen?

What if we'd been high school sweethearts who followed each other to college?

What if she and I had gotten married instead of me and my ex, who turned out to be a soul-sucking narcissistic barracuda of a woman. I did have a beautiful daughter from the relationship, but her mind had been so poisoned with lies about me by her mother that I hardly saw her, maybe once a year at most.

Maybe Zara and I would have had children together?

Maybe we would be well on our way to growing old

together, and I wouldn't be living this nightmare with my mother. Or at least I wouldn't be doing it alone.

I'd made so many mistakes, and I still hadn't learned. I didn't deserve someone like Zara Fowler Ames. But there was something I could do to help her with her situation at work. At least I hoped it would.

I planned to put my newly acquired writing skills to work this weekend and at least try to make up for some of the pain I'd caused.

Zara

I walked out of the police station absolutely stunned. Not only had Shea turned over the recording of my conversation with Alan the night before to campus police, which they passed along to city police, but between that, my affidavit and Ana's, it looked like Alan was finally going to be held accountable for his crimes.

"Did he really think he could get away with this?" I asked Ana as we headed to my car. We were headed straight back to campus, so we rode together.

When she looked at the ground, I realized what I said was a huge mistake. "I'm sorry, Ana. I didn't mean to suggest you were wrong for not fighting back, for not going to the authorities. What you said about the dean, the president and the good ol' boys network makes perfect sense. I'm just lucky we have a new dean now..."

"Why'd you tell the police about your affair with the student?" Ana changed the subject. "I wouldn't have disclosed that if I were you."

I bit my bottom lip as I thought about it—because I surprised myself too when I blurted it out mid-interview. "I guess I figured if I was going to do this, accuse Alan of harassment, blackmail, assault, and all that, then I wanted to do it with a clear conscience. I will deal with the consequences of my choices, and I'm fine with that. Guess I might be looking for a new job soon."

Ana nodded. "I hope not, though. You're a great professor, and they'd be crazy to let you go. Every one of your intensive writing students I end up seeing in a 400-level class is a way better writer than the ones who had someone else."

"Um, you mean Alan?" I laughed. He was the other professor who taught intensive writing, and because of his chair duties, that was the only class he taught anymore. Two sections, and that was it.

Since my divorce, I'd taught an overload—three sections of first-year composition, one intensive writing, and a poetry class. They didn't have too many English professors who were willing to commit to that much grading.

I parked in the faculty lot, and Ana and I walked back to our building. Clouds were gathering to the west, and it was only a matter of time before rain pelted campus. Hopefully the storm would pass before I had to return to my car.

"Thanks for going with me today, Ana, and sharing your story. I think it helped a lot." I opened my arms. "Do you mind if I hug you?"

A bright smile spread across my colleague's face as she nodded. "I'm glad I was able to help, and that I had an opportunity to talk about what happened with someone. But best of all, I think justice will finally be served."

"Amen!" I agreed as I squeezed my arms around her

petite frame. I left her outside her office and walked down the hall to my own.

Nothing looked like it had been touched since I left, but I had the brief, wistful memory of seeing Shea in my doorway as he said goodbye. We agreed to stay away from each other for the rest of the semester. He'd still be in my class, but I'd have to interact with him just like I did every other student.

It was the right decision—if I was even allowed to carry on the rest of the semester. But I wished there was another way. I still didn't understand everything that happened when we were teenagers, but I knew he didn't purposely abandon me at the office building downtown last night. His recorded evidence corroborated my story, and it was one of the major reasons Alan was being held.

I wonder if he'll make bail?

To counteract the creepy shudder that racked my body when I considered Alan walking around a free man, I imagined how amazing it would be to have Shea's strong arms around me right now. My pleasant reverie was interrupted when a new email pinged on my work account. As soon as I saw it was from the dean's office, my heart skipped a beat, and my stomach plummeted.

Zara –

In light of what happened with Alan and your student, I feel we need to have a conversation. Please plan to meet with me in my office at 8 am sharp Monday.

Regards,

Cheryl Silva

Word sure travels fast, I thought as I replied to her email to let her know I'd be there. It was time to face the music.

* * *

Over the weekend, in the midst of a frenzied grading spree, I took a few long moments to really contemplate my life choices. *Maybe I'll just become a crazy cat lady and live frugally off my savings until I die of loneliness*, I thought as I scoured the freezer and fridge for something edible. I didn't expect anything to taste good, and I wasn't even hungry, but dinner seemed like the right thing to do.

I slumped on the sofa while I waited for my microwave meal to heat up. How much more pathetic could I actually get?

I thought about my hospital visit—was that really only two days ago now? It seemed like such a blur, but some parts were so vivid, like the flashbacks I had as Floating Me. That homecoming dance felt so real, I could practically smell the Drakkar Noir the boys around me were soaked in. The sounds of Nirvana and Foo Fighters were ringing in my ears. Laughter and snickering echoed in the caverns of my mind as I remembered the glittering tiara being stabbed onto my head by Mrs. Pastorelli.

I was a queen without a king. And everyone was gossiping about what happened to Shea Hunt. How did I block out this memory for so long? Why did I remember that something happened to him, but I couldn't remember what?

The microwave was dinging, but I was starting to slip back into the past, my consciousness wavering as I teetered on the edge, taunting the ghosts that had been haunting me for nearly twenty-five years. And just like that, I snapped out of it, knowing what I must do.

Grabbing my phone, I took a deep breath as I headed to Facebook and typed *Jenny Birt* into the search bar. I was only friends with a couple people from high school—teachers. They were in their sixties, seventies and eighties now, but many of them were still kicking.

And there she was: *Jennifer Birt Price*. She was married now, and she had a friend in common with me: our senior year English teacher. When I pulled up her picture, I knew immediately it was her. Her eyes were smaller, with dark circles underneath, and she had a couple of laugh lines around her mouth, but it was definitely my friend from high school, one of two friends who were with me at the homecoming dance that night.

With trembling fingers, I hit the button to message her. I typed, "Hey, stranger! Is this Jenny from Jefferson class of '96?"

I set my phone down to retrieve my meal from the microwave and settled back in on the sofa with the bowl of noodles, wishing it was something I actually wanted to ingest. Before I could take a bite, my phone buzzed. Jenny had messaged back.

Jenny: *OMG is that you, Zara Fowler? I don't know any other Zaras <laughing emoji>*

Me: *It's me. How are things?*

Jenny: *Going well. One kid in college and one a senior in high school.*

Me: *Wow! How did that happen?*

Jenny: *Well, it has been twenty-five years. <laughing emoji>*

Me: *True. I can't believe it.*

Jenny: *Going to the reunion next summer? I'm on the planning committee.*

I'd never been to one of our class reunions. I couldn't imagine that would change now, but I wanted Jenny to talk to me. I was warming her up for an important question I wanted to ask, but I didn't want to just blurt it out abruptly.

Me: *I'll definitely think about it.*

Jenny: *Your profile says you're a professor at State. Congrats!*

Crap! I didn't even look to see what she's doing now.

Me: *Yep. Pretty fun job, for the most part.*

Now was my opportunity. Just go for it.

Me: *Hey, I was thinking about our senior year homecoming since it's been twenty-five years this month. Do you remember that night?*

Jenny: *Wow, I certainly haven't thought about that night for a long time. I know you weren't very happy about what went down at the dance...*

Me: *No, but I'm coming to terms with everything slowly.*

Jenny: *That's good.*

Easy for her to say. *Sigh.*

Me: *I was wondering if you remembered what happened to Shea Hunt that night, why he didn't show up.*

Jenny: *You don't remember? <shocked face emoji>*

Me: *What do you mean?*

Jenny: *Well, it wasn't a good night for Shea either...*

Me: *What happened? I don't know why I don't remember—I think I blocked it all out.*

Jenny: *Zara...Shea's twin sister Caroline was hit by a drunk driver that day.*

Me: *OMG, really? I didn't know he had a twin.*

Jenny: *She was a special needs student—she went to a different school. She was waiting to be picked up at her school because she didn't drive, and while she was waiting for her ride, sitting on the curb, a drunk driver hit her. She later died.*

Me: *Wow. I had no idea. How did I forget that?*

Jenny: *I don't know. It was all over the school by Monday. Shea was gone that whole next week.*

Zero memory. I had absolutely zero memory of that. But I did remember that after the homecoming dance, he left me alone. I didn't remember having any interactions with him after that night.

Me: *Thanks for letting me know, Jenny. I feel awful that I forgot.*

Jenny: *I don't know what made you think of that night all these years later. I hope everything is okay.*

Me: *It's not now...but it will be.*

I left Jenny hanging on that cryptic message while I slurped down the rest of my noodles and then grabbed my laptop from the armchair. I searched *Caroline Hunt*, our town name, and the month and year of the accident.

I really didn't think anything would come up, but there was an article in our local newspaper. By luck, it wasn't behind a paywall.

I scanned the article, my heart pounding when I read about the horrific accident that happened at the Harold P. Inman School. Reading further, I gasped when I came to the absolute worst part: the identity of the drunk driver who struck Caroline Hunt.

Michael J. Hunt.

Seventeen

Shea

MONDAY, I got home from work late and only had time for a two-hour nap before I needed to head to campus. The last thing I felt like doing was seeing Zara—at least class wasn't until tomorrow, so hopefully I wouldn't run into her today. I wasn't sure what happened after I left her office. All weekend I fought off the almost irresistible urge to call or text her to see how she was. I hadn't been able to get her off my mind. Why, after all these years, was I still so obsessed with her?

Because that's what it is: an obsession.

I'd wanted her since high school, and I behaved like an absolute idiot. The fact that she knew and got past it somehow to even speak to me, let alone make out with me... I didn't know what to make of it. I didn't deserve it. Especially after I let her down with Alan.

Let her down?

Hell, I'd completely failed her.

I looked in the mirror, steamed up from my scalding hot shower. As if I could burn some of the guilt away.

I had planned to apologize to her after homecoming, actually. I didn't know that my friends were going to humiliate her when they meant to humiliate me. They are the ones who had everyone write in her name for Homecoming Queen and vote for me for King. They thought they were pulling a prank on me. But then everything happened with Caroline and—

"Michael?" called my mother from her bedroom. I needed to get her up, serve her breakfast, help her dress and get her situated in her chair before I left for campus. Judy would finally be able to look in on her at lunchtime.

I'd fucked up as a brother. I'd fucked up as a son. I'd fucked up as a decent human being.

Hopefully I would be able to make it through the rest of the semester, earn passing grades and be accepted into business school. I wanted to finally make something of myself. Finally get a chance at not being a fuckup.

I knew the Alzheimer's Foundation in the city was going through an expansion, and in three to five years they would be looking for an executive director. I knew this because the current executive director was one of my mother's doctors, and he was being spread too thin with his medical practice and working for the foundation. It was a part-time position now, but with the expansion, it was going to become a full-time position that required an MBA or a master's in public health policy or administration. My university didn't have a graduate health policy or administration program, so I really hoped an MBA would suffice.

Doctor Jessup told me as soon as I completed my business degree, I could start working there in the grants office or outreach department—whichever I preferred. I was on the right track, but I needed to get into the business school and finish my degree in the next two years if I was going to make this happen.

I wanted it more than anything.

Well, more than almost anything.

Right now Zara was at the top of my list.

Too bad that wish was way out of my reach.

Zara

My stomach felt like a nuclear plant had a meltdown inside it as I rode the elevator to the dean's office in the administration wing of our building. The dean was scary smart, had an impeccable memory and fiery tongue, and had already proven herself able to drink anyone under the table at holiday parties.

I stopped outside her office, nodding to her secretary. "I'm here to see Dean Silva."

"She's expecting you," the petite brunette informed me with a sympathetic look—like she knew I was about to get blown to smithereens. "Go on in."

With trembling fingers, I twisted the doorknob and entered the dean's inner sanctum. She sat behind her desk, all bright-eyed, dark braids coiled around her head like a crown. I supposed if she got angry they may turn into Medusa's snakes?

"Hi, Zara," she greeted me, sounding almost pleasant. I knew her well enough to know she could turn on a dime. Last semester, a philosophy professor got fired for sexually harassing the administrative assistant, and rumors about Dean Silva's utter ruthlessness spread like drunkenness at a frat party.

I took a seat when she gestured toward the leather chair across from her desk, which was a highly polished cherry. These pieces were so much more refined and classier than my own office furniture, but I supposed that was just one of the many perks of being dean.

"I wanted to assure you first and foremost that Alan Palmer is no longer employed at this university," she began our conversation.

I couldn't begin to describe the immediate relief I felt. The old cliché of a giant, hulking burden being lifted off one's shoulders was in no way adequate, and though I was a poet, I refused to take a stab at finding a better metaphor. I bit back stinging tears with sharp teeth stabbing into my lower lip as the dean shuffled some papers on her desk.

"I know about you and your student, Shea Hunt," she continued.

My breath hitched. She fired Alan, and she would fire me too. I could almost feel the heat of the coming flames.

"I'm going to be honest with you, Zara, I did consider some sort of punitive action because, as you know, we have a zero tolerance policy against professor and student fraternization at this university." Her dark eyes flashed at me with a warning, but then softened.

"Considered?" I stammered.

"I was prepared, when I sent you that email, to suspend you without pay for a number of weeks and to deny your tenure," she admitted.

My lungs squeezed as I gulped down a breath. "But something changed your mind?"

She nodded. "Yes. I received this. I want you to read it."

My hands were shaking as the paper she handed me fell into my grasp. I could tell right away it was a printout of a message sent through our school's email program. My heart raced as I read:

Dear Dean Silva,

I hope it's okay that I'm contacting you. I found your email on the university website. I'm writing about a professor in the English department, Dr. Zara Ames.

I know Dr. Ames is meeting with you, and she and I both suspect you have heard some rumors about us having a relationship. First, I want to say the rumors are true. Dr. Ames and I have had a physical relationship this semester.

But I want you to know the rest of the story before you judge her or punish her in any way.

First of all, Zara and I have known each other since high school, where I bullied her about her weight. The truth is I had a mind-blowing crush on her back then, but I was too embarrassed to date her because my friends would make fun of me.

I feel positively awful about the way I treated her and was completely flabbergasted to discover she was my professor for intensive writing this semester. I thought about transferring to a different section, but because of my job and some family obligations, hers is the only class that will work for me.

Here's the absolute truth: yes, I've had a physical relationship with Dr. Ames this semester, but I have also learned a great deal about writing: style, mechanics, grammar, syntax, argumentation, citation. The reason I've learned so much has nothing to do with my feelings for Dr. Ames. I've learned so much because she is a gifted teacher. She's tough, but her methods work. Just ask any student in our class if they've become a better writer over the course of the semester, and I know the answer will be a resounding yes.

The reason I was so eager to take this class is because I am trying to get into the business school this spring semester, and the one requirement I still need is intensive writing. I want to finish the bachelor's degree I started decades ago so I can go on to get my MBA and work for a nonprofit in the city that is dedicated to helping Alzheimer's patients.

I feel like most of my life I've been a fuck-up—pardon my language, but it's honestly the best word choice, and if there's one thing Dr. Ames has drilled into my head, it's proper word choice! I was let go from my last job because of my anger and authority issues. I've always had these issues, which is why I'm overstepping my bounds now, and probably why I seduced my English professor.

Did I mention I've been a fuckup? I am responsible for my sister's death and consequently my father's suicide. I'm not responsible for my mother getting Alzheimer's, but I am responsible for taking care of her, and I failed to do so the other night when Dr. Ames was trying to ensnare her boss in a trap to prove he was blackmailing her and coercing her into performing a sex act in exchange for her tenure confirmation. I was supposed to rescue her at the last minute and couldn't because my mother took the wrong medication, fell, and had to be rushed to the hospital.

I want nothing more than to finish this class, get my degree, enroll in graduate school, and get my dream job to finally be in a position to help people instead of constantly fucking things up. Like I said, I need this class to do that.

However, if it means Dr. Ames is going to be

suspended or terminated because of her inappropriate relationship with me, please, I beg you, let me be the one to drop the class or unenroll from the university.

I care too much for her to let her suffer because of my bad choices, and I am definitely the one who instigated our relationship.

If you'd prefer to speak with me in person, I am happy to meet with you. I can answer any question you'd like as to Dr. Ames's fitness to continue teaching at this university. You really owe it to all of her students to keep her on. She is the best teacher I have ever had, and I'm not saying that just because I'm in love with her.

And if this argument isn't enough, feel free to check out her recently published volume of poetry. It's pure brilliance, Dean Silva. Check it out. I'm sure you'll agree.

Sincerely,

Shea Michael Hunt

I set the paper face down on her desk as a tear slipped down my cheek. I whisked it away, hoping Dean Silva hadn't seen it, but her hawklike stare had been pinned on me the entire time I was reading.

"Is that all true?" the dean asked, the corners of her lips curling up ever so slightly.

I nodded. "Well, the parts about us knowing each other since high school and him bullying me... I really do try...as far as teaching goes."

"I'm not going to fire or suspend you, Zara," the dean said, her eyes bouncing between mine. "Though there is something you can do for me..." Her eyebrows arched as she reached over to the bookcase beside her desk.

My heart skipped a beat when she brought out a hardcover edition of my poetry book and set it on the desk. *She owns my poetry book?*

"Can you autograph this for me?" she pleaded. "I have to tell you, I'm a huge fan of your work."

I was utterly speechless as I took the pen she offered me. Turning the pages, I settled on a spot to sign my name, then I finally let out the breath I'd been holding for what seemed like the past forever.

I left her office feeling like I must be suspended in a dream.

There was no possible way that could have gone any better than it did.

And Shea was in love with me?

Shea

I was sitting in my econ class when my phone buzzed with a message. The professor was mid-lecture and had a strict no phones policy, and I wasn't about to screw up another class. So I ignored it. Even when it buzzed again. I really hoped it wasn't Judy with some sort of issue with my mother. No, she would have called—and I would have stepped outside to take it.

As soon as class ended, I whipped out my phone to see that my two missed texts were from Zara. My heart thundered in my chest, and a lump swelled in my throat as I brought up the messages.

Zara: *I need to see you.*

Then, ten minutes later:

Zara: *Please? It's urgent.*

She needed to see me. *It's urgent,* she said. What if she got fired, and she wanted to say goodbye?

Was it wrong that for a fleeting moment, I selfishly fantasized about her termination meaning we could be together?

Ha! Like that would even be an option for her.

I texted back on my way to my next class.

Me: *I thought we weren't supposed to be talking outside of class?*

Zara: *Meditation room?*

I sighed. I had an exam next hour. One I'd barely studied for because I'd spent so much time writing an email to the dean and poring over it with a fine-toothed comb. I didn't want to have any grammar mistakes or typos— anything that would negate my claim that Zara was the best teacher I'd ever had.

Me: *I have an exam next class.*

Zara: *What time are you free?*

Me: *3*

Zara: *I'm in class then. What about 3:45?*

Me: *I won't have long. Need to be home by 5.*

Zara: *Can you give me 15 min? I need to talk to you in person.*

Me: *okay*

* * *

Praying I didn't just bomb my exam because I couldn't get my mind off Zara, I paced all over campus trying to kill the forty-five minutes I had to wait. At 3:40, I rushed across campus to the chapel. The small building was quiet as usual, though there was a student kneeling at the altar with her hands clasped together in prayer. I stealthily slipped past her to the meditation room door.

My breath caught when I slowly pushed it open and took Zara in, stretched out on her side on the giant floor pillows. She was a vision in a deep, saturated shade of emerald green. Her dark hair was falling in her face, obscuring one eye, while the other met mine with a sultry gaze.

I seemed to catch her off-guard because she startled when she realized I was actually standing there. "Interrupting something?" I joked.

She sat up, her cheeks flushing. "Sorry, I was just remembering the last time we were in here."

I extended my hand and pulled her to standing. "Ah yes...I don't recall getting a lot of meditation done that day."

She smiled and wrapped her arms around my waist. "I had to see you."

My eyebrow quirked. "You did?"

"I met with the dean today, and she let me read your letter."

"Oh yeah?"

She nodded, her lips spreading into a huge grin. "Shea, not only has your writing improved a great deal since we first met, but—"

Now I was nervous. I didn't pull any punches with that letter, and yet I meant every single word. If she didn't return my feelings, my heart was going to shatter.

Then again, I didn't deserve her forgiveness. Her love.

Not after bullying her in high school and then letting her down the other night.

Remembering that, I pulled out of her embrace and took a few steps back, my heart sinking down low in my chest. Sure, she was in a good mood now—her job was safe. But she couldn't actually have feelings for me—not the kind of feelings I had for her.

"What's wrong?" Her dark brows arched as she held my gaze, her chest rising and falling with rapid breaths like she was nervous to have this conversation.

"Zara, I—" I closed my eyes and swallowed hard. "I...I needed to write that letter, but—"

"But what? You didn't mean it?" She nodded, her smile slowly fading before turning into a frown. "Right. Of course. You were just trying to help me keep my job."

"No!" I corrected her. "No, I meant every single word; it's just... Zara, I don't deserve you. What I've done in the past is unforgiveable. I've hurt you. All I *do* is hurt people. And I don't want to hurt you anymore—as much as I want to be with you. As much as I—"

"Shea," she cut me off, "that's not for you to decide, you know. I should get a choice. I did some research into that night twenty-five years ago—homecoming night. It wasn't your fault that your friends nominated me for home-coming queen, and you for king, and then got everyone to vote for us. And it's not your fault that you didn't show up that night."

"You know about that?" I blinked a few times, searching her face for the truth.

Her eyes filled with pain. "I know what happened to your sister..."

I blew out a breath as I stepped away again, this time turning to face a giant tapestry woven with a Biblical scene. It was one of sheep on a hilly countryside, and the words "The Lord is my Shepherd; I shall not want" were embroidered in gold thread. I was supposed to be my sister's shepherd. I failed her.

"No..." I swallowed hard again, wishing I didn't have to tell Zara the truth about me. About my family.

"No what? You lost your sister." She came up behind me and placed her hand on my shoulder. "I had no idea. I blocked out everything that happened at school that next week, I was so upset about the dance. I blocked out the whole dance, for that matter! I only remembered you asking me to it...until the memories came back when I was in the hospital after my...after the thing with Alan."

"I never told anyone what actually happened," I confessed, my eyes still glued to the tapestry. "If you heard something, it was just a rumor that was going around the school."

"I looked it up in the paper," she explained. "I read the article about your sister getting hit by a drunk driver."

"A drunk driver that was my father," I said, my voice low.

"I read that too." She sighed as she put her other hand on me and tried to turn me to face her. She couldn't move my body herself, not until I willingly spun to meet her imploring gaze. "It's not your fault, Shea. You didn't deserve to have that happen in your family. I know you're taking good care of your mom, and—"

"No." I shook my head. "No, that's not the whole story. It *was* my fault. It was *all* my fault."

She was still staring at me, a look of confusion spreading across her face. "You're not a fuck-up, Shea. I know your letter to the dean said that, but it's not true. You're a kind and caring man. You're taking good care of your mother—"

"It's my fault she is the way she is," I snapped. "I made her that way."

"It's not your fault she has Alzheimer's, Shea. That's ridiculous!"

"Is it?" I bit back. "I was supposed to be the one to pick Caroline up from her special school that day. I was supposed to be there at three-thirty. But I got caught up helping with our class float for the homecoming parade. It got to be three-thirty, and I was angry at my parents for expecting me to take care of my sister when they were perfectly capable of doing it themselves. But apparently my mother was getting her hair done, and my father was where he was every afternoon after work—the bar."

"That's not your fault," she tried to soothe me.

"Don't you understand?" My voice shook as my throat filled up with emotion. "I just decided not to go. I thought to myself, fuck them. It's my senior year. I should be able to hang out with my friends after school instead of having to pick up my stupid sister. I was sick of them making me take care of her, be responsible for her."

I scrubbed my hands down my face. "I was going to say it wasn't my fault she was born with special needs, but, yeah, it kind of fucking was because we were twins, and I apparently sucked up all the nutrients or some shit, I don't know. I was completely normal, and she always had problems. So I guess it *was* my fault she had special needs."

"So you didn't pick up your sister," Zara surmised.

"Right. And when I didn't show up, Caroline's school secretary tracked down my father, who said he would come and get her. Well, he came all right. Drunk as a fucking skunk. Drove his truck right up on the curb and ran right over her."

"Shea..." She reached out for me, but I ignored her, pacing to the door.

"He fucking killed her. But it should have been me who

picked her up, right? It was supposed to be me. Then a few years later, my father blew his fucking brains out. My mother was never right after that. Sure, they diagnosed her with Alzheimer's, but it was Caroline's death that started her spiral downward, and my father's suicide only drove the nail into the coffin. She had no chance after that."

"It's still not your fault your father was drunk. And it's not your fault your sister had special needs," she insisted.

I looked down at my watch. "I've gotta go. I've gotta get home to my mom. I'm glad the letter worked, and you get to keep your job, Zara. I won't expose our secret tomorrow in class. So don't worry about that—"

"Shea, please," her voice carried down the hall after me as I left the meditation room.

This was for the best.

I would be able to finish out the semester. We'd keep things professional. I'd earn my passing grade with hard work, and I could move on with my life.

Maybe someday I would even get that redemption I'd dreamed about.

Eighteen

Zara

MY HOUSE FELT SO empty when I returned, but I could still hear Shea's voice echoing in my ears. I still saw the pain etched on his face when he spoke about his family. He had a troubled childhood with a special needs twin sister, an alcoholic father, and a mother who was...well, I didn't know if she was always checked out, or if she just couldn't handle the burdens thrust upon her shoulders. But Shea shouldn't have had to bear the weight of his father and sister alone.

I sat down on my sofa, exhausted from the roller coaster I'd been riding all day. My cat jumped up beside me, nuzzling into my hand to demand some attention. There was something so soothing about stroking a pet's fur, but I couldn't get my mind off Shea.

I was falling for him. Hell, I *had* fallen for him. And there was no way I could let him go on believing he wasn't worthy of me, of forgiveness, of having a happy life just because his family situation was so messed up.

He might have had authority issues in the past, but he was trying to do the right thing. At forty-two years old, he was trying to make a fresh start and do good in this world. He may have felt like he needed to atone for the pain he'd caused others, but whether or not that was required, he was in the position to do a lot of good for millions of Alzheimer's patients and their families.

I couldn't just let him go.

Not without helping him realize that he truly was a good person, even if he had a hard time believing it. I would give him some space for now, but I hoped to show him how much potential he had.

* * *

The next day, I stood at my instructor station and talked about my rubric for grading the midterm essay comprising twenty-five percent of each student's grade in the course. The final would be twenty-five percent as well, and all the other papers and assignments amounted to the remaining fifty percent of the final grade. I had to keep the numbers simple being a word person and not a math person.

"Now that we've gone over that, I have something special I want to do in class today." My eyes spanned the classroom, where my twenty-six students sat hanging on my every word. "Some of you may know I'm a poet. It's a bit of a departure from the usual essays we write in this class, but I wanted to do something fun in this last class before fall break, and also issue you a challenge for over the break. This is purely for extra credit, so feel free to opt out. But I think you will find it a lot of fun."

I'd managed to pique their curiosity. A lot of widened pupils stared back as I scanned the room, their eyes bright and questioning. *And some of these kiddos definitely need extra credit!* I mused.

"We're going to write a special kind of a poem. It does not need to rhyme—in fact, it's better if it doesn't. Yours can be any length, but the idea is for the message to express one sentiment when you read it from top to bottom, and then if you invert it and read the bottom line to the top line, the sentiment is exactly the opposite. This is called a reverse poem. I wrote an example to share with you."

I swallowed hard as I pulled up the other document I'd opened on my instructor station. Looking out across my students' faces, my gaze briefly landed on Shea. He locked his eyes with mine for a moment and then glanced away as soon as I began to read. I hoped I could bring him back with my poem—because I wrote it for him.

"I really do
Hope you know
No one could love you
After what you've done
So don't try to tell me
You can start over
There isn't any hope for a person like you
No one will say
You can redeem yourself
Your mistakes
Are more important than
Your best efforts
Give up now
I'm telling you don't
Try to change

Your future is dim unless you
Realize
You're right where you belong."

"Wow, that's stone cold, Dr. Ames," one of my students
blurted out, and everyone snickered.

I smiled, not letting the comment bother me. "But now
let's read it in reverse, okay?"

Shea's eyes dropped to the desk, where they stayed until
the very last stanza of my poem.

"You're right where you belong.
Realize
Your future is dim unless you
Try to change
I'm telling you don't
Give up now
Your best efforts
Are more important than
Your mistakes
You can redeem yourself
No one will say
There isn't any hope for a person like you
You can start over
So don't try to tell me
After what you've done
No one could love you
Hope you know
I really do."

Shea

A hush fell over the room as Zara finished reading the poem she wrote, and by the way her gaze kept flitting to me, lingering away then snapping back, I knew it was written for me. Could this beautiful woman have found a more beautiful way to show me how she felt about me? *I think not.*

The way her eyes sparkled as she delivered the last line... I was sold. All I could think about was taking her back to the meditation room and showing her how much I liked her poem with my hands and lips. How was I going to wait another forty minutes?

Once the spell she cast over her students wore off, a wide grin spread across her face. "I'm going to email you the poem for inspiration, and if you want the extra credit, just email me your own poem by the end of break. Any questions?"

She glanced around the room, but no one said a word. Each and every student still seemed to be in awe. "Great. Then I'm letting you go early today. Enjoy your fall break!"

A wild cheer roared through the room as if she'd just declared we were having a party, then everyone started to gather up their belongings and filter out the door. I slipped a tiny note on Zara's instructor station before heading out.

Meditation room in 10, it said.

My walk across campus in the brisk fall sunshine was a moment of joy I wouldn't soon forget. I'd had a heavy burden on my shoulders—and I still did. It wasn't like my mother was going to magically recover. But I had a goal of finishing my degree, and the next stepping stone was getting into business school. For the first time this semester, I was confident it was going to happen.

But it was more than that. I had someone who believed in me, who believed I was a good person capable of great things. And that was more valuable to me than anything, because it was something I always wanted but never had.

When I got to the chapel, there was no one inside. Soft organ music piped through the speakers as I walked down the main aisle of the sanctuary. They must have had a CD playing because no one was sitting at the small organ.

I slipped inside the meditation room and sucked in a huge whiff of incense. The tapestry with the sheep and a Buddha surrounded by candles on a small table in the corner greeted me. A bookcase near the window held volumes on finding inner peace, reconciliation with estranged family members, and Christian baptism. A cross hung on one wall next to a Star of David and another symbol I thought might be Muslim. I liked how they went to so much effort to make this space inclusive as the chapel was billed as nondenominational.

After some time passed and the music looped to the mystic pan flute and nature sounds from our first visit, I checked my watch. It had been almost twenty minutes.

Maybe she wasn't coming?

But she wrote that poem.

She couldn't have written that poem if she didn't believe it, just like I couldn't have written the letter to her dean if every word wasn't true.

She wanted me to believe in myself. That I was deserving. That I was forgiven, and that I was worth someone caring about. I'd told myself for so long that I wasn't, but how could I be unworthy when a woman as incredible as Zara Fowler Ames had fallen for me?

Just then, the doorknob twisted, and a familiar pair of eyes met mine.

"That was some poem," I broke the silence.

"It's a lot harder to write a reverse poem than I thought it would be!" She laughed. "But I figured I wasn't much of a poet if I couldn't figure it out."

She started to ramble on about her poetry abilities, when I stepped forward, cupped her face in my hands and claimed her mouth. Heat seared my body as my tongue parted the seam of her lips and delved inside, her body melting into mine as she succumbed to my kiss.

"My god, Shea," she finally said, breaking apart from me, her mouth glistening.

"I've been such a fool," I said. "First, treating you the way I did all those years ago, like you had no feelings, when I really just wanted you, to know you, to have a chance with you. Secondly, feeling sorry for myself for the fate I resigned myself to and wallowing in self-pity over the guilt I felt. I knew I had a chance to start over—but I don't think I really believed I deserved it until you came back into my life."

Her eyes crinkled as she took me in—there might have been the shimmer of an unshed tear in the corner of mine. "It sucks what you did and what happened to you, but it doesn't have to define you. You don't have to punish yourself for the rest of your life."

"I realize that now, but I don't think I would have ever gotten there on my own, so thank you for that."

"I was still that timid, self-conscious fat girl," she continued. "But I'd puffed myself up on all my academic accomplishments, girded myself with self-righteousness and indignation over the way I'd been treated by men. I never thought I'd find someone who accepted me as I am."

"As you are? You're beautiful and brilliant," I chuckled. "The best of both worlds." I took her into my arms again and stroked my finger down her cheek, flinging away a tiny teardrop that had escaped from her eye during my speech. Not one of sadness, not the type of tear I made her cry twenty-five years ago, but one of joy.

"I want to make love to you, Zara," I told her. "Not here, not in the meditation room. Someplace where I can linger over your beautiful naked body and worship every inch of you."

"But you have work...and your mom..."

Nothing had ever felt more right than this. I wanted to show her we could make this work. "I know. So let me take you on a real date as soon as we can schedule one, and then spend the night with me."

"At your house?" Her eyebrows quirked.

"Yes. My mother will be there, but she's not there, you know? She sleeps..." I started to apologize about my situation, but she pressed her finger to my lips.

"If we're going to do this, I know she is part of the deal," she interrupted me. "I am okay with that. I want to help in any way I can."

This beautiful creature was an angel on earth. "Thank you for that." My heart was swelling with love for this woman, and I wanted to tell her how much she meant to me, how badly I wanted to make her happy, but I wasn't a poet like she was. There was no way I could ever find the right words.

I would have to show her with every touch, every kiss, every embrace.

Nineteen

Zara

SHEA and I finally got our date the following weekend. He took me to his favorite Italian restaurant, and we both scanned the place first to make sure we didn't recognize anyone from campus.

"The dean didn't actually tell me to stay away from you," I told him, laughing when I realized we were both doing the same thing. "She told me she trusted my judgment."

"Dinner with a student isn't so scandalous, anyway, is it?" His turquoise eyes twinkled as he reached across the table to cover my hand with his.

"Hardly scandalous at all!" I agreed. "What comes after dinner though..." I waggled my eyebrows.

"What do you think our high school classmates would say if they saw us now?" he asked me.

I let out a long sigh. I had blocked out a lot of my high

school memories, so purposefully thinking about it felt strange. "They'd probably take credit for trying to hook us up at homecoming."

He chuckled, a hearty laugh coming straight from his belly. "You're probably right, those assholes."

"I wonder what would have happened if you *had* shown up at homecoming that night..." This was the first time I ever allowed that question to take up space in my mind.

"I don't know," Shea answered honestly, "but I hope I would have danced all night with you and not given a fuck what anyone thought. Seventeen-year-old Shea was such a dumbass."

"Seventeen-year-old Zara wasn't exactly the smartest either...but I had potential."

He squeezed my hand. "Just like I do now."

I nodded and smiled at the server when she returned with our wine. After she uncorked the bottle and poured our first glasses, Shea took his and held it up. "Here's to us —and our potential."

I raised mine and clinked it against his. "To our potential."

* * *

His neighbor, a retired nurse, took care of his mother when he wasn't able to, and he'd asked her to feed his mother dinner tonight while we were out and help her get into bed. When Shea opened the door to his small bungalow, it was quiet and cozy, no sound but the hum of the refrigerator. I wandered into the living room, my gaze immediately falling on dozens of photos arranged on the walls.

"Is this your...?"

"My daughter. She lives on the West Coast."

"She's beautiful!" I gasped, staring at the blonde with turquoise eyes like her father's.

"Thanks. And that's my mother and father's wedding photo." He pointed to a very 70s-looking bridal party in a silver frame. "And this is my mother when she was younger."

"Well, it's easy to see where the family's good looks come from." I took a few more steps inside, my eyes trailing over the plethora of sci-fi and fantasy books on his shelves. He was a reader. That made my heart go pitter-patter.

"Thanks. It's hard to see her go from that to..." He started to get choked up.

"Hey..." I wrapped my arms around his waist and laid my head on his chest. He blew out a breath and relaxed into my embrace.

"You're right. It's not what I wanted to share with you tonight. Will you come with me?" He held out his hand.

"Anywhere..." I took it and followed him down the hallway to the last room. Surprise sent goosebumps rippling up and down my arms as I surveyed the space. LED candles glowed from multiple levels: the nightstand, the chest of drawers, and some decorative shelves, bathing the room in soft light. He pressed a button, and slow classic rock flowed out of speakers on either side of his bed. Three vases of flowers infused the space with an exotic, tantalizing scent.

"This is amazing, Shea." I turned to face him, and he captured my lips with his own.

"I want to give you so much...the world..." he whispered as he bent to plant tiny kisses along my collarbone. Goosebumps erupted again, this time over my whole body, as he trailed them up my neck to behind my ear. "I can't yet, but please be patient. I'm working on it."

"All I need right now is you," I assured him, drawing his gaze to me so he could see the truth in my eyes. "Just the fact that you're willing to put forth effort...I'm not used to it." My ex ignored me most of the time. I hardly even felt like I was married. But I didn't want to talk about or think about Brandon tonight.

"You're going to get my very best," he promised, slipping my dress over my head. "I'll never stop making up for what I did..." He bit his lip as he took in my lacy bra and panties set.

The desire in his gaze was undeniable and sparked a shiver down my spine. "You don't have to make up for anything. You just need to show me you care." It was more than I'd ever gotten from anyone else.

"I intend to do that and so much more." He guided me to the bed and gently lowered me to the mattress, his strong arms wrapped around me. "My god, you are just so breath-taking. Every inch of you is divine. You're not just a poet, Zara...your whole body is poetry."

A flush bloomed on my cheeks and spread across my chest as he reached around me to unclasp my bra. "This is lovely, but I want to see you...all of you..."

I sucked in a breath as he whisked the lacy bra away and my full breasts bounced back against my ribcage, sliding to their respective sides of my body. He scooped them between his large, strong hands and bent to delicately trace a circle around each nipple with the tip of his tongue. Somehow he knew just how to tease them to almost painful agony, and my whole body was quivering by the time he decided to move on to other unexplored areas.

My core tightened, and when he spread my legs and the air hit my panties, I knew they were soaked. He hooked his thumbs in each side and slid them down my thighs. The heat of his breath fell on my mound of curls as he breathed in my essence. "Fucking nectar of the gods right here, Zara..."

He was still dressed at this point, but I wanted to see and worship his body too. I sat up and reached for the hem of his shirt. Smiling, he slowly, teasingly unbuttoned the shirt and tossed it aside, exposing the thick mounds of his pectoral muscles, covered in dark hair with a few silver strands glistening in the low light. His muscles rippled as he climbed off the bed to remove his jeans. He left his black boxer briefs on, but the outline of his hard cock was unmistakable.

"I've been wanting to taste you ever since the last time," he confessed as he climbed back between my thighs and slowly lowered his mouth to my throbbing clit. After nuzzling his mouth against my lips and teasing them open with his tongue, he lightly stroked it against my swollen numb, causing the ache in my core to deepen.

I'd never had a lover who took his time exploring my body. They'd always been so focused on their cocks and what I could do to get them off. Having someone slowly savor and devour me was new—and I loved every minute of it.

The attention to detail, the absolute precision of his mouth, tongue, and fingers all working in perfect synchronization to drive me to the absolute brink of insanity were astounding. Even as a poet, I could never capture with mere words the heights to which I soared when I finally released.

"Fuck, you're drenching my face, Zara!" His voice was garbled by a gush of juices as my orgasm rocked through me.

"Fuck me," was all I could say as I started to come down from the high.

He slid up my body, a grin on his glistening face. "Happy to oblige." Then his eyes rolled back in his head as his thick cock pushed inch by inch inside me, stealing not only my breath but any coherent thought I might have formed.

He rocked into me, his hips meeting mine in a slow rhythm as the last spasms of my climax squeezed him. He gasped as he reached up to clasp his hands in mine. "If you keep doing that, I'm not gonna last long."

"You think I can control that? Fuck, it's your fault anyway..." As I started to laugh, his lips found mine, and he swallowed down the beginning of my giggle, turning it into a raspy moan as he pumped into me a little faster.

"I always wondered if it would be like this with you," he confessed when his eyes met mine. "I had a feeling, behind that shy exterior..."

"You thought about having sex with me?" I knew he'd liked me when we were younger, but—

"Um, I used to jerk off thinking about you all the fucking time, Zara." He sighed. "Even after the disastrous homecoming night."

"But you left me alone after that..."

"Doesn't mean I wasn't thinking about you."

There were so many what-ifs about our past, but I didn't want to dwell on those. All I wanted was for my man to explode inside me and set off a chain reaction in my body, one that made me tumble over the edge right after him.

"God, you feel so fucking amazing, I don't ever want it to end," he finally said after my thoughts came full circle back to the bed, where he was still driving into me, his face creased with concentration as he attempted to hold himself back.

"Then don't let it end..." I moaned as he hit my G-spot and I gushed around him again. I was fairly certain my inner thighs and his balls were coated in my juices now, and there was going to be one hell of a wet spot by the time we were finished.

"I don't plan to ever stop loving you," he growled, biting his lip as his eyes snapped shut in ecstasy.

"You love me?" My voice was soft, hopeful. He'd said as much in the letter to the dean, and I'd said as much in my reverse poem...but we hadn't yet said the words in person.

"I do, Zara... I love you, and I don't ever plan to stop."

"I love you too, Shea, and if you *do* stop... then...I'm going to publish a whole volume of revenge poetry about you," I ground out between thrusts.

"Holy fuck, well, we can't have that, now can we?"

"Come inside me, Shea." I grasped his stubble-flecked jaw in my hands. "Tell me you love me and come inside me."

"Only if you come with me." His demand was raspy and sharp around the edges with his flinty breath falling on my cheek.

"Yes...please..." I arched my back, taking him somehow deeper as my legs wrapped around his waist. "Just like that, Shea..."

"Yes, ma'am." His thrusts became faster, more intense as we both chased our orgasms, our bodies grinding against each other like perfectly crafted gears.

"Oh, god, Zara, are you close?"

"Yes," I moaned.

"Come with me," he groaned seconds before an unintelligible string of words and curses exploded out of his mouth. His body stilled, and in that moment, my body knew exactly what to do. My core clenched, and the waves of ecstasy crashed over me, drowning us both in pleasure.

As he held my quaking body in his, he whispered in my ear, "Now, just one more question remains..."

The seriousness of his tone made my body stiffen. "What's that?"

"Will you go to our twenty-five-year reunion with me?"

Epilogue

Shea

Nine Months Later

THE SUMMER SUN soaked into our bare skin as we headed back to the hotel to get ready for the reunion tonight. Zara's new convertible was a bright spot of fun in what had been a stressful month. She'd gotten the keys just days before my mother took a turn for the worse. This week, we said our final goodbyes, and yesterday was her funeral.

We already had tickets for the class reunion tonight, and Zara told me right away that she would be okay with us canceling. But since we lived only an hour away from the small town where we'd gone to high school, and we'd

179

already gotten a room for the evening so we could stay out as late as our now forty-three-year-old bodies would allow us to, I insisted we go.

Besides, I'd been planning for this night ever since our first official date nine months ago, when we exchanged our first "I love yous" and made love in my bed for the first time.

"You sure you're okay to go tonight?" She stroked her finger down my bristly cheek as soon as she put the car in park. She hadn't let me drive her new baby yet, but I figured it was only a matter of time before I convinced her to hand over the keys.

"I told you a million times I'm ready for a night out," I insisted. We'd been through a lot this month, and we both deserved to blow off some steam. Not that class reunions didn't come with their own sort of stress, but I figured we were both pretty eager to show off our relationship to our classmates.

"There are sure going to be a lot of whispers and head shakes tonight," she said. "We can always stay in and order room service if you'd rather."

I grasped her hand in mind and squeezed. "How many times do I have to tell you? I'm ready for tonight. I'm excited. Besides, I want to see you in that gorgeous dress and show you off to all our friends."

"Your friends," she corrected me.

"I know you have a little bit of trepidation about the prank they pulled our senior year...and I don't blame you. If you're having second thoughts, we can—"

"No," she cut me off. "I was only worried about you. I'm a fucking doctor, Shea. I have a published book of poems and another one in press. I am a tenured faculty member at the state university. Plus I have a hot-as-fuck boyfriend. I've got nothing to be ashamed of. If anything, I'm the ugly duckling who grew into a swan."

"You were always a swan to me...and I'm sorry I made you think otherwise." I leaned down and kissed her cheek. I didn't know if the guilty feelings would ever go away.

She'd told me a million times she'd forgiven me. I would give almost anything to go back in time and do it all over again, and Lord knows I'd make other, better choices as well. Like picking up my sister and taking her wherever she needed to go.

But it didn't do any good to dwell on the past like that, which was what Zara always said. "We can only move forward." That was her motto. And I had adopted it as my own.

Zara

The music was thumping from the end of the hall as we made our way to the hotel's ballroom, where our reunion was being held. Balloons in our school colors danced on strings above the registration tables. After greeting our classmates who were manning the table, we both leaned down to sign ourselves in and collect our nametags. Shea grabbed mine right away.

Where it was printed, "Zara Fowler Ames," he took a Sharpie and wrote "DR." in front of it.

"Here, fixed it!" He handed it to me with a grin.

This man was incorrigible! Even though his lack of

respect for authority had gotten him in trouble a time or two in life, I sure was glad he'd helped me stand up to my authority figure, Alan Palmer. He had been released from his contract at the university, and, as far as criminal charges were concerned, he pleaded guilty to a lesser assault charge so he didn't have to face me on the witness stand in the courtroom. And you know I would have destroyed him even further than he destroyed himself.

When Shea and I walked into the reunion, hand in hand, unsurprisingly, every head turned in our direction, and more than a few jaws dropped. We were arriving fashionably late because we may or may not have gotten caught up in some extracurricular activities back in our room...

"It's so good to see you!" A lady with a blonde pixie cut and wearing a purple dress rushed up to me and threw her arms around my neck. "I'm glad you came."

I beamed at my old friend Jenny Birt, who still had the same toothy grin as when we were kids. "Thank you! Jenny, do you remember Shea Hunt?"

Her eyes widened as she took in Shea's broad form in his sports jacket and dress shirt, no tie. "I do remember you —kind of surprised to see you two together."

"Well, let's just say we've put the past behind us," I said with a grin. Shea nodded in agreement, then whipped around when someone clapped his back from behind.

"Hey, guys, it's Three-Point Shea!" shouted a deep voice.

"Ton' the Clone, great to see you, man!" The two men did the one-arm hug thing, and then a few other friends of Shea's ambled up, and we all acknowledged each other. Two of the men had their wives with them, while two others were flying solo.

Jenny was also flying solo, and I immediately noticed

one of the guys checking her out. Maybe something would happen there?

I was pleasantly surprised at how gracious everyone I spoke with was. Shea wandered off with his buddies for a little while, which was fine. I liked that we weren't attached at the hip. Several of my classmates told me they had my poetry book on their shelves. I could hardly believe anyone knew I'd even published a book, but the fact that they'd bought it too? How incredible!

I was in the middle of a conversation with two people I knew from drama club when there was a commotion at the DJ booth. I heard, "You can't have the mic. I'm in the middle of a rotation!"

"Oh, god," Scott Pierson rolled his eyes, "that's Shea Hunt, isn't it? He hasn't changed a bit. He's trying to wrestle the mic away from the DJ."

With a sick feeling growing in the pit of my stomach, my eyes darted over to the corner where the DJ was set up. Sure enough, Shea was having a heated conversation with the man, who was young with spiky green hair and arms full of tattoos.

"Shea always had a problem with authority, didn't he?" Cassandra Diaz agreed as she scoped out the situation.

I hadn't told Scott and Cassandra that I was dating Shea, so my mouth just snapped shut as I watched the scene unfold. Finally, the DJ threw up his hands and exited the booth, relinquishing control of the microphone to Shea.

The music faded out a few beats later, and Shea's raspy voice filled the room. "Good evening, Class of '96! How's everyone doing tonight?"

Some whoops and cheers went up from the audience. I gave an uneasy clap as I waited to see what he would say. *If he embarrasses the shit out of me...*

"I don't know if anyone remembers homecoming our senior year, but I had an unfortunate accident in my family and was unable to make the dance. I found out later I'd been crowned homecoming king, and that Zara Fowler had been crowned queen. So I went through some old video footage of that night and learned that the song we should have danced to was 'Tonight, Tonight' by The Smashing Pumpkins. I'm going to start that song right now," he pressed a few buttons on the DJ's laptop as the DJ ran anxious hands through his green spiky hair, "and I'm going to ask that you all indulge us in the dance we were supposed to get over twenty-five years ago."

Everyone around me pressed their hands to their hearts and let out a collective, "Awww."

"But one thing before we get started..."

The first strains of the music welled up as he unhooked the microphone from its stand—thankfully it was cordless—and began to step toward the dance floor. Jenny appeared out of nowhere and urged me to join him. My heart was thundering inside my chest as I slowly stepped toward him, teetering in my heels as my lungs fought to take in air.

Shea made it to the edge of the dance floor and dropped to one knee. The audience's "aww" became a breathy gasp.

Suddenly there was no one else in the room. Just Shea with his gorgeous turquoise eyes, scruff-lined jaw and kiss-able lips. And me, struggling to keep my lungs working as I waited to hear what he would say next.

"Dr. Zara Fowler Ames, not only was our night ruined all those years ago, but I was a huge jerk to you in high school. The fact that you've forgiven me is more than I could ever ask for, but I'm a greedy asshole, so I'm gonna ask you for one more thing."

He swallowed hard, then looked up at me with love and hope in his blue-green eyes. "Will you marry me?"

My heart pounded even harder, and I really thought it might just burst right through my ribcage as I looked down to find him balanced on one knee, holding a small velvet ring box in his hand. When he opened it, diamonds caught the light like an exploding firework, and my hands flew to my mouth in shock.

Words eluding me, all I could do was nod as he slipped the ring on my finger and pulled himself to standing. His arms wrapped around my waist as we swayed to the song we should have danced to together all those nights ago. Twenty-five years of nights ago.

"Our night was ruined, and I was a huge jerk back then," he reiterated, his eyes locked on mine as the diamond on my finger glittered in the swirling dance floor lights. "But I want to spend the rest of my life proving to you that we belong together. I love you, Zara."

Who could have foretold that our paths would cross again and bring us to this moment? Who would have ever thought I could forgive this man, let alone fall in love with him? It could only be our destiny, sealed by my ability to forgive and his beautiful promise to never stop proving his love to me.

Words stolen along with my breath, the poet in me could only choke out, "I love you too, Shea." Then I melted into his embrace as his lips found mine and we danced our way into forever.

THE END

* * *

Want more steamy romances? Join my Facebook group for games, giveaways, and sneak peeks!
www.facebook.com/groups/PhoebesAngels

Or join my newsletter here:
https://bit.ly/PhoebeAlexanderNews

USA Today Bestselling Author Phoebe Alexander writes sexpositive bodypositive erotic romance featuring compelling plots intertwined with passionate, fiery encounters. She believes that real, relatable characters can have even steamier sex than billionaires, rock stars, and the young and lithe-bodied. She also advocates for ethical non-monogamy through her writing.

Phoebe lives on the East Coast of the US with her husband, sons, and multiple fur babies. When she's not writing, she works as an editor and consultant for indie authors. She also volunteers her time running a 6000-member indie author support group. Her sexual fantasies have all been fulfilled, and now her single greatest fantasy is just having some damn free time.

Also by Phoebe Alexander

Mountains Series
    Mountains Wanted
    Mountains Climbed
    Mountains Loved
    Christmas in the Mountains
    The Navigator
    The Explorer
    The Adventurer
    Mountains Transcended

Eastern Shore Swingers Series
    Fisher of Men
    The Catch
    Siren Call
    Sailors Knot
    Turning the Tide

Spicetopia Series
    Sugar & Spice
    Virtue & Vice
    Fire & Ice
    Naughty & Nice
    Dares & Dice
    Loyalty & Lies

Spice Up Our Marriage Series
    Project Paradise
    Rule Breaker
    The Playground
    Keeping Secrets

Alpha Bet Guys Series
    A Hole
    The Big O
    Need the D
    Hard F
    Ride the C